THE
BABY PLAN

An uplifting feel-good romantic comedy

EMMA BENNET

Previously published as *Her Sister's Baby*

JOFFE
BOOKS

Revised edition 2024
Joffe Books, London
www.joffebooks.com

First published in Great Britain in 2021 as *Her Sister's Baby*

Cover art by The Brewster Project

ISBN: 978-1-83526-519-2

For Ally.
One of my absolute favourite people in the whole world.
I'm sorry I cut the fringe off your Barbie
because she was prettier than mine.

x

PROLOGUE

The road was deserted, illuminated only by the beams of her headlights stabbing out, piercing the thick, encompassing darkness. Her mind was a maelstrom of emotion and her cheeks wet with tears. Anger was dominant; at the situation, but mainly at herself, and she realised she was pressing down on the accelerator far too aggressively and needed to slow down. She gently eased the pressure on the pedal.

The dashboard display showed it was just after 11.30 p.m. But she wasn't tired. Running on adrenaline, she was determined to right some wrongs tonight. Even if that resolution hadn't gone well so far. The past . . . well, she'd made a lot of mistakes in life. Hurt too many people. It was time she made amends for what she could.

This wasn't how she'd planned to spend her evening. By this time she'd usually be tucked up in bed, her little girl asleep in her cot at the end of it. But she'd be back home, back with her precious daughter, in a few hours.

She glanced across at her bag on the passenger seat, needing, at a deep level, to triple check the letter was still poking out of it. It had been hard to write. And impossible to send. She'd had it for ages, re-reading it, rewriting it, trying to find the words to ask for forgiveness. In-person, she thought she'd flounder, freeze up or say the wrong thing, that her intentions wouldn't be believed. And who could be surprised at that? She'd gone between giving up on the whole thing, then gathering her resolve. So, she'd decided to put things down on paper. But afraid of being rejected, she hadn't been brave enough to send it.

She was going to do this, she reiterated like a mantra. Today. Now. She'd felt she should at least take it in person. Atonement in some way.

She looked back at the road. Christ! She hit the brakes as hard as she could, instinctively yanking the steering wheel and swerving violently to avoid the black cat fleetingly registered in that sliver of a second, dead ahead in her path.

Too much, too late.

The car drove straight off the road and smashed into the barrier.

CHAPTER 1

Sophie was in such a deep sleep, it took a little while before she came to and realised the telephone was distantly ringing. Her mobile on the nightstand showed 01:17. Sleep fogged and as disorientated as she was, her heart immediately began thumping faster, her body instinctively reacting with fear to a call in the middle of the night.

She stumbled out of the tangle of bedclothes and hurried into the hall, the slight chill of night air unheeded. Rubbing her eyes, she found the handset and answered with a cautious, "Hello?"

"Is that Sophie Perring?" asked a tired, flat female voice.

"Yes."

"I'm a nurse calling from the Royal Sussex County Hospital." A pause. "Your sister, Natasha, has been in a car accident."

Sophie felt herself take a sharp intake of breath. "Is she OK?"

"I'm afraid not, she's in a very serious condition." There was another second's pause before the nurse continued, her matter-of-fact tone tinged now with sympathy, "You should get here as soon as you can."

"I'm on my way," Sophie said automatically, already making a mental plan of how to get to the hospital. Now the phone had delivered its crushing news, strangely her heart ceased pounding, an empty iciness freezing it, and her stunned emotions were in place. She felt on the precipice of a vertiginous drop, not daring to feel lest she lose all control and fall. She had to focus on getting to the hospital, to Natasha.

Quickly, Sophie pulled on a pair of jeans and a hoodie onto her small 5'2" frame. She found trainers, then tied back her shoulder-length brown hair. She clumsily grabbed her mobile, purse and car keys and was out of the door only a few minutes after putting down the phone.

She hadn't visited Natasha in Brighton since her sister had moved down there a couple of years before, and wasn't familiar with the route. Thankfully the sat nav flawlessly guided her through the ghostly London suburbs and away from the security of her little South Norwood flat. The further coastward she went, the lonelier Sophie became as the sparse number of her fellow nocturnal travellers dwindled to nothing in the dark open countryside; leaving just the odd pair of headlights glaring in the opposite lane. She futilely tried to divert her spiralling panic by wondering what their stories were — happy? Sad? Mundane?

No hour and a half journey had ever taken so long, it felt.

She pulled into a space at random in the largely empty hospital car park, her breath quickening painfully. An irreverent liturgy of 'Oh Christ, oh Christ,' filled her thoughts, accompanying each reluctant, queasy step in the walk to the Accident and Emergency Department. She headed in, everything other than the reception desk subconsciously blocked out.

"My sister was brought in a couple of hours ago, her name's Natasha Perring," she heard herself blurting out.

Did she imagine the wash of pity flooding the receptionist's face? Had this woman even got any idea who Natasha was as she replied, "Take a seat love, I'll send someone over."

Sophie did as instructed and sat down on a hard, plastic orange chair. She contemplated getting a coffee from the vending machine in the corner both from habit and to occupy herself, but knew it would be dreadful. And perhaps caffeine wouldn't be the best idea in her current shaky state.

Her foot tapped uncontrollably on the floor. She focused on it intently, not wanting to make eye contact with anyone. Her emotions contained completely within herself.

"Ms Perring?" she heard and looked up. A young female doctor was in front of her, shapeless in ill-fitting scrubs. Her face and eyes too carefully expressionless.

"Yes."

"Would you mind coming with me?"

Sophie followed the doctor through a set of swing doors, along a dreary, antiseptic-smelling corridor and into a small, empty consulting room.

"Take a seat," suggested the doctor, gesturing towards a chair behind Sophie.

"I'm all right standing," Sophie responded, despite the sudden shaking which had taken control of her.

The doctor took a moment before speaking again, her tone soft but professional, the delivery measured but clipped. "Natasha's car came off the A23 outside Brighton and she drove into the crash barrier soon after midnight. There was no one else involved, but Natasha's internal injuries were extensive. She was unconscious when she came in, but we were able to identify her from items in her purse, and you were down as her next of kin. She didn't suffer and would have been unaware of what was happening. She never regained consciousness, and I'm afraid she passed away a little while ago."

Sophie's legs gave way beneath her. She instinctively grabbed hold of the chair and sank down into it. In that moment her body processed what her mind couldn't: giddy, trembling, her senses shrinking in; her thoughts froze, void of comment. It was too much. How? Why? It couldn't be right — it couldn't be! A mistake must have been made

— Natasha had to be alive. It had to be someone else. But as much as she longed to, she couldn't fall for the comfort of her own desperate lies.

"Would you like to see her?"

Sophie managed to somehow nod her agreement.

"If you'd wait here, I'll get someone to take you."

Sophie sat, motionless, her entire being trying to take in what had happened in the space of a few hours: her sister — her only living relative — was gone. The only person who remained who'd known her for the whole twenty-seven years of her life. They hadn't been close for years, hadn't even seen one another for an awfully long time, but, none the less, Sophie felt a terrible, heart-rending loss, as if she were totally alone in the world. Trapped in her pain, the tears came.

Eventually, a nurse knocked tentatively and entered. Sophie half smiled in reflex when he introduced himself, automatically going through the rituals of polite society despite what was happening. Trancelike, she was led down numerous corridors, none of which she paid any attention to until they stopped outside a closed room.

"Take as long as you need," the nurse said, holding open the door for Sophie to pass through.

She stopped at the threshold, gathering her resolve and trying to calm her racing breathing and trembling limbs again. One gut-wrenching step at a time she walked slowly in, only able to approach the shrouded figure on the bed by dehumanising her, focusing solely on the indistinct, amorphous contours of the drawn-up hospital sheet. By detaching herself from the situation.

She barely registered the, "Come out to the nurses' station down the hall if you need anything," as her escort slipped away.

The bed was surrounded by a huge assortment of medical equipment, all still in disarray and dumped on a selection of trolleys. Everything was turned off now. Despite the hour, vague, distant 'busy' noises filtered through to her. The constant soundtrack of hospital life.

Finally, she gazed down on her big sister's upturned face. She seemed . . . peaceful. There were cuts to her cheeks and forehead, but she must have been cleaned up because it didn't look like she'd been in a major car accident, and certainly not one that could have caused her death. What had she even been doing driving towards London at that time of night?

It was clichéd, but Natasha could easily have been asleep, Sophie thought. Her skin was pale but still flushed with health and vitality. It'd been maybe three years since they last met but, relaxed and still, Natasha now seemed the younger of the pair, far younger than her thirty years, the one in need of protecting. Part of Sophie expected her sister's eyes to pop open at any moment and for her to ask where she was and why Sophie was staring at her with tears running down her face.

She was sobbing she realised; deep, shuddering, primal sobs.

Remorse coursed through Sophie: she and her sister may have been polar opposites in so many ways, but Natasha was the only relative Sophie had left. Maybe she should have done more to put the past behind them and work on a relationship with her sister. But there was nothing to be done about that now, and that knowledge, and the regret that went alongside it, was very hard to deal with.

Sophie tentatively leant forward and stroked Natasha's long, blonde hair, "Goodbye," she said quietly.

There was a soft knock at the door. "Come in," croaked Sophie, wiping the tears away with her sleeve.

The door opened and a large, motherly nurse came in.

"If you could follow me to the desk and show me some ID, there's paperwork to go through and I've got Natasha's belongings for you."

"Could I have another minute?" asked Sophie.

"Of course, darlin', take as long as you need."

* * *

Sophie walked to the reception desk, where she signed forms in a daze, the bureaucracy of life not stopping even now. She was handed a large carrier bag full of the possessions found with Natasha.

"There's a mobile phone in there that's been ringing non-stop," a nurse said. "I'm afraid we had to switch it off."

She remembered to thank the nurses for everything they'd done but left as soon as she was able to, wanting to be alone. She took some time to compose herself on a bench outside the Accident and Emergency entrance before she got back in the car to drive home.

Remembering what the nurse had said, she turned on Natasha's phone. The pin code was Natasha's birthday, the numbers she'd always used. At least that was something she knew about her sister, Sophie comforted herself.

The phone started ringing almost the moment it was switched on, Sophie automatically answered it.

"Where are you?" hissed an angry woman's voice before Sophie had a chance to speak. "You said you'd be back by eleven. I had to bring our Jade and the baby to mine. And she won't settle, will she! It's gone four! Jade's got school in the morning. She never would've babysat if she'd known you'd bugger off again with some bloke. You haven't done a runner have you?"

"Sorry, who is this?" asked Sophie, perplexed.

"Natasha?" questioned the woman.

"No, this is her sister."

"Where's Natasha then?"

Sophie couldn't bring herself to speak the words to explain her sister was dead.

"Fine," said the woman, impatiently, a baby's piercing wail had started in the background. "Where are you?"

"I'm outside the hospital," Sophie found herself responding.

"Well, you've got fifteen minutes to get here and pick up your sister's baby, or I'm calling the Social."

"Her *baby*?"

"I'm not kidding. Fifteen minutes."

"Where are you?"

"15b Rodney Street."

The woman put down the phone.

"What the . . . ?" thought Sophie staring at Natasha's mobile in disbelief: Natasha had a child? When? Her sister was *a mother*? She was an *aunt*! And she'd had no idea. Grief, confusion and deep, deep sadness rose up from inside her and the sobs began again. She struggled to suppress them. Now wasn't the time. While it was too late to repair things with Natasha, she did have a new-found niece, her sister's baby. Another chance of sorts. She had to get to her.

But who, and where, was the father? She drew a long breath in, and forcibly exhaled. She needed to focus. She had some sympathy for the poor woman on the phone, still up at 4 a.m. dealing with a squalling baby. She'd sounded very fed up, and while she had no doubt the threat to call social services was an empty bluff, she didn't want to exacerbate the situation.

Taking her own mobile from her pocket, she googled the address — it was only about twelve minutes away: even factoring in the time getting to her car, she should be there in time.

* * *

Slowing down to check the name on the road sign caught in the headlights, Sophie drew up to the curb as her sat nav announced, "You have reached your destination". In the glow from the street lamps, uniform blocks of flats lined both sides of the deserted road.

As Sophie approached the building housing 15b, she saw the front door was wide open and the lights on in the hallway illuminated a broad, heavyset woman with short, blue hair, holding what at first glance appeared to be a bundle of clothing, but on second look was a baby.

The woman stomped down the path and dumped the child and a bag into Sophie's arms.

"Alana's had her formula. Tell Natasha that's the last time Jade or I help her out. Her keys are in the bag. If there was ever a kid who needed a father, it's this one. She's a crap mother. Believe me, I know what it's like to be bringin' up a little one by yourself, wantin' a bit of time to be free, but that Natasha . . ."

Sophie tried to interrupt, "The thing is, Natasha . . ."

"I don't want to hear any of it. I've tried to help her, the ungrateful cow. Well, I said never again and I mean it."

"Natasha . . ."

"I'm not interested."

In the face of the continuing brusque hostility, Sophie swallowed her awkward words of explanation and, clutching her precious package, turned to go. "Twenty quid is what Jade was promised," said the woman, impatiently tapping her foot and holding out her hand. She made no attempt to mute her voice despite the hour and her presumably sleeping neighbours.

Sophie managed to move the baby so she could hold her in one arm, with the bag in her other hand, she managed to extract her purse from her handbag. The woman didn't offer to help as Sophie struggled to open the purse and extract two £10 notes.

The woman grabbed them and flounced back up the path, shutting and loudly locking the door to the block of flats behind her.

Sophie let out a deep breath and stared down at the child in her arms. So, Alana was her name. She seemed wide awake, though silent now. She had blonde hair and piercing bright blue eyes. She stared seriously at her aunt as if taking her in as much as the other way around.

Sophie automatically began to walk back to her car, and it was only when she'd opened its doors that she realised she didn't have a car seat for Alana or any idea where she was planning to drive to. She couldn't go back to her flat in London without being able to take her niece in the car, and even if she could get there, what would she do with a baby in her flat? She wouldn't have anywhere for Alana to sleep even.

Despite the early hour, it was warm even for July and a definite blush of orange was beginning to lighten the horizon. Needing some time to think, Sophie took the bag of Natasha's possessions off the passenger seat and headed downhill towards the sea, hoping the sound of the waves would soothe her and the baby, who'd begun to grizzle and wriggle in her arms. It wasn't far.

She found her way to the coastal wall, then made it onto the beach very gingerly, terrified of dropping Alana as she navigated the uneven stones. Managing to sit down fairly comfortably, Sophie held Alana close to her and wrapped her in a little blanket that had been in the bag of Natasha's things, maybe it would smell of her mother and be a comfort to her, as well as keeping her warm. Natasha, a mother. She stared down at her niece, amazed at how familiar her bright, intense gaze seemed, even though they'd only just met. Alana closed her eyes and fell asleep. Sophie didn't dare move in case she disturbed her.

She already felt very protective over the tiny person in her arms, the only part of her sister she had left, the only part of her family, and she instinctively needed Alana to be with her. It didn't seem the little girl had anyone else either.

She looked out over the water. It was timeless. Fresh, clean, beautiful. The foam crests of the waves formed and broke, endlessly trapped in a cycle of death and rebirth — symbolic perhaps, Sophie thought. Natasha was gone, too late now to heal their rift. How sad, now, in the face of the ultimate truth of things. But here in her arms was a form of second chance, solace perhaps for them both. An end, too, of her well-ordered life and an abrupt induction into chaos she suspected, but that couldn't be helped.

Gulls cried and circled, raucous over the soporific chant of the sea.

She needed an immediate plan and some sleep. Everything else would be dealt with as she needed to. Her organised, meticulous inner-self — the consummate planner/strategist — rebelled at this disorderly cop-out, this was not how Sophie

Perring functioned, but she overruled it. Taken as a whole, she'd be overwhelmed by what faced her. It was . . . too much. Too alien, too many unknowns. Sleep and small steps — that was the only way forward.

She carefully extracted one of her hands from under Alana and looked through what she'd been given by the disgruntled babysitter. There were a few baby things: a cuddly grey rabbit, a bottle with a tiny bit of milk in the bottom, some wet wipes and a nappy.

Next was the carrier bag of Natasha's belongings. Knowing that putting this off wouldn't help, Sophie let out a sigh before opening it. Inside was a striped canvas tote with a long shoulder strap: Natasha's handbag. Her purse was in there, house keys, some make-up, and a couple of Final Demand notices. As the first letter was only dated a few days ago, she presumed the address on it was Natasha's current home address. She gently teased her mobile out of her pocket, never taking her eyes off her niece in case she was about to wake and start crying. She again googled the address and, to her huge relief, it was a few minutes' walk away, two roads down in fact from Rodney Street where she'd been so recently. Wondering whether Natasha had a flatmate or, unlikely as it now seemed, a boyfriend living with her — though if she did, especially if the boyfriend were Alana's father, surely the hospital would have called him instead of her? — Sophie decided to head to the address. If they did exist, they'd have to be woken up.

She was putting the letters back in the bag when another unopened envelope caught her eye. She pulled it out and saw her name written on the front. Cack-handedly tearing it open, she drew out a single sheet of paper covered with her sister's unmistakable scrawl.

Dear Sophie,

Thank you for taking the time to read this. I thought it better to write because I know I won't be able to find the words in person, and I wasn't certain how you'd react to seeing me. It's been a long time, and I'm sure you're still angry with me for the way I've acted in the past. I treated you and Mum and Dad very badly, and for that, I'm very sorry. I was selfish, and I know I hurt you all, but I have changed, and I want to try to make amends if you'll let me. We're the only family either of us has, except for someone I'm dying to introduce you to. I have a daughter, Alana. She's seven months old. I understand if you don't want anything to do with me, but there's nothing more important than family and I so want you to be a part of my and Alana's life. Please get in touch.

Love, Natasha.

A mobile number was written on the bottom of the page.

Natasha must have been travelling to deliver the letter; the hospital had said she was driving out of Brighton, Sophie realised. She'd been on her way to Sophie's flat to try to make amends. If only she'd completed her journey, if only they'd had the chance to reconcile, put the past behind them, and become proper sisters again.

Sophie somehow got up while still holding the sleeping baby and packed up the bits she'd pulled out from the bags. She stood up straight, trying to instil within herself the self-assurance she wasn't feeling at that moment and allowed herself one long, final survey of the sea.

"I'll always look after her, Natasha. I promise," she said out loud, "I'll take care of your daughter."

CHAPTER 2

Sophie was woken a few hours later by the sound of Alana crying in her cot at the end of the bed. She struggled up, exhaustion coursing through her, as she checked the time on her phone. It was just gone nine o'clock, which in regular circumstances she'd consider a very decadent lie-in, but she hadn't climbed into Natasha's bed until almost six and had lain awake for at least another hour listening to Alana sleeping, going over and over what had happened until her nervous energy ran out and fatigue overcame her.

Natasha's home had been empty when she'd reached it. The flat had its own front door onto the street and was on the ground floor of a large, blockish, modern building. Sophie noticed the space was small and messy, but she hadn't bothered to examine it properly. She'd been shattered and had put the baby straight into her cot before changing into a pair of pyjamas she'd found in Natasha's chest of drawers and going to bed herself after emailing the accountancy firm she worked for to let them know there had been an emergency and she would need to take some time off.

Sophie picked up her niece and it was immediately obvious, even to someone who knew practically nothing about babies like Sophie, that Alana needed her nappy changed.

There was a changing mat on top of the battered-looking chest of drawers in the corner of the room and a few minutes later, Sophie was proud of the job she'd done, even if she'd had to hold her breath the entire time. The baby certainly smelt an awful lot better but was, unfortunately, still crying.

"I guess you're hungry as well," said Sophie, trying to stay calm and think through the steps of what could be making Alana unhappy. She grabbed her indispensable phone from the bed and carried Alana through to the little galley kitchen, googling on the way what she should feed her. It seemed it depended on how much a seven-month-old had been 'weaned' as to what they ate, which didn't really help matters. Formula seemed a safe bet, and she found a box of it on the counter, along with a steriliser. She peeked inside the machine and found there were clean bottles. She read the side of the formula packet. The instructions seemed clear enough, but it would take a while before the milk was ready for Alana, and she didn't sound willing to wait.

Sophie really needed her morning coffee. She took a deep inhalation; it was hard to concentrate with a baby screaming in her ear. She spotted a highchair in the corner of the kitchen and managed to strap an extremely indisposed Alana into it so she could at least use both hands and not worry about spilling hot water on her niece.

She almost had the bottle prepared, when Sophie heard the doorbell ring over the sound of the crying. She went to answer it, only remembering as she reached the kitchen door that she couldn't simply leave the baby alone — goodness knows what could happen! Getting frazzled, she lifted her niece out of the highchair, which seemed to make Alana crosser than she'd been when she was originally put in it.

The doorbell continued ringing, becoming more insistent, forcing Sophie's blood pressure to soar even higher. The sheer number of locks and chains on the front door reminded Sophie her sister's neighbourhood was perhaps not as salubrious as her own. There was no peephole, so she opened the door gingerly, ready to slam it shut quickly if necessary.

What faced her could have been the god Thor, or perhaps someone from the cast of an Australian soap opera. One who worked out. A lot. At least 6'2", lean, very tanned and muscular, with shoulder-length, wavy blond hair. He wore a faded T-shirt and board shorts despite the fact the day hadn't heated up yet. He, rather incongruously, held a pink teddy bear in his hands. Sophie met his eyes, which were the intense blue of the sea on a cloudless summer's day. She felt herself feeling hot all of a sudden. Her examination was brought to an abrupt halt by his wince as the full force of the baby's crying hit him.

"Is that Alana?" he asked, not taking his eyes off the baby, which Sophie was quite glad about as she was sure she looked an absolute state.

"Who are you?" she asked, politely, forcing herself back to the reality of a stranger standing on the doorstep enquiring after her niece, but, bizarrely, not recognising the baby.

"Is Natasha in?" he responded.

"Are you a friend of hers?" Sophie questioned. Was it her imagination, or was this guy being deliberately elusive? And why did he seem so fascinated with the screaming child in her arms? — his attention still hadn't left her.

"You could say that," he answered after a pause. "I'm Samson. Alana's father."

Shocked, all Sophie could think of to say was, "Oh." Having been told there was no dad in the picture, she hadn't truly considered Alana having a father. She'd been too fixated on the immensity of events, and functioning moment to moment, to give it any more thought yet.

"So, is Natasha here?" Samson asked again.

Finding the words difficult, Sophie took her turn at being evasive. "If you're Alana's father, why didn't you recognise her?"

Things didn't quite seem to fit together here she realised. Subconsciously she held the child closer, already unknowingly feeling a fierce maternal instinct towards her.

Samson's piercing blue eyes rose to properly meet hers, and she almost wished they hadn't as they weighed her in silence for a moment.

"If you must know, I've only met Alana once before. Very briefly. I . . . didn't get to see her properly." He scanned her face. "You're very like Natasha, are you her sister?"

Sophie nodded in affirmation, emotion stifling her voice.

"I'm assuming she didn't tell you that I didn't even know she was pregnant," he continued, clearly taking her lack of comment as judgement and anxious to justify himself. "She only told me about Alana last night, when she brought her to my house, and then she ran off. I've been trying to call her mobile, but it's going straight to voicemail, so I thought I'd try here. Is she around?"

"You'd better come in," said Sophie, opening the door fully. She was aware she knew nothing about this man. But he seemed honest, or at least direct — which may or may not amount to the same thing she mused — and surely no one would make up a story like that.

They stood uneasily in the hall, Alana still screaming incessantly and Sophie trying to think how to word what she needed to tell him.

"Why is she crying?" Samson asked.

"She's hungry. I think. I was in the middle of getting her bottle ready. Would you hold her for me for a minute?"

Samson appeared a little alarmed, but accepted Alana. "This is for you," he said gently, handing her the teddy bear. She took it from him and clung to it, but didn't stop wailing.

Sophie added the scoops of powder to the water she'd poured into the bottle as quickly as possible and tested it on her wrist like she'd seen someone do somewhere — possibly in a movie — to check it wasn't too hot.

"It seems ready," she said, thankfully, and Samson handed Alana back to her. She held the bottle out to Alana and the little girl grabbed hold of it, popped it in her mouth and began drinking greedily, stopping crying immediately. Sophie and Samson both heaved a grateful sigh.

Again their eyes met, but Sophie quickly glanced away. "I'm sorry, what's your name?" he asked her.

"I'm Sophie."

"Is Natasha here?" he said, determinedly repeating his earlier question. "It's really important I speak to her."

"No, she's not," said Sophie, and took a deep breath before continuing. "Um . . . There isn't a good way of saying this. I'm guessing you guys weren't particularly close right now, but . . . um . . . so . . . Natasha was killed in a car crash last night." The last part came out in a rush, the words almost tripping over each other.

"What?" Samson's face lost all its colour as he processed what she'd said.

"I don't know the details of how it happened yet," went on Sophie, trying to keep her voice steady and her rapidly welling tears in check.

Samson was quiet and stared down at his feet; startled and bewildered at the news.

"That's awful," he said finally. "I'm so sorry."

"It's OK," muttered Sophie.

"Was Alana in the car?"

"No, she was with a babysitter."

"Thank goodness," Samson commented. "What happens now? With the baby?" he continued rhetorically. He ran a hand through his hair, thinking. Unhappily he asked, "So, who do I get in touch with?"

"What do you mean?" replied Sophie.

"Well, who do I need to inform?"

"About Natasha dying? No one. She died in hospital, it's all being taken care of. I've signed anything that needed to be signed."

"No, no. About Alana. As her dad, I guess it's down to me. Do you know who I should contact to let them know where she'll be living? I suppose I should take her now," he rambled, clearly dazed by the enormity of what he felt confronted him, but determined to step up.

"Alana's not going anywhere," said Sophie, firmly. "She's had more than enough upset in the last twenty-four hours. She's staying here with me right now — I'm her aunt, she doesn't know you. You had no idea she existed until yesterday."

Technically a day ahead of me, she added internally. She was maybe being unfair. She understood, at least a little, of what must be going through his mind, but her desire to care for Alana was disconcertingly strong. She knew it was right, especially after reading Natasha's letter. She was sure it was what her sister would have wanted. Neither she nor Samson had known Natasha's secret or been there for Alana for the first months of her life. But she was there now, and she would protect and love her niece as well as her mother would have. She and Alana needed each other. She didn't know a thing about this man. Other than that her sister had presumably chosen to be a single mother.

"I'm her father. She's my responsibility."

"You're not taking Alana anywhere," Sophie reiterated. "She's staying with me."

"You have no right to do that," he said, voice rising with his temper.

"My sister was Alana's mother."

"And I'm her father."

This was all too much for Sophie to deal with, too much upset and confusion. She needed this man gone so she had time to think and work out what she was going to do. She somehow had to learn how to look after a baby and completely reshape her life around her. There was no way she could add in some random chap who'd turned up claiming to be Alana's father to the equation. And she couldn't even contemplate giving up the only family she had left.

"How do I know you're telling the truth?" said Sophie, defensively, though deep down there was no doubt her niece and this man were related. All Alana's features, from her hair to her chin resembled his. And anyway, what a bizarre ruse for him to pull if he were lying, why would he want to do it? The only logical explanation was that this man was Alana's father, the repercussions of which were huge.

"I'm sorry, but I have no idea if you're actually who you say you are, you have no proof, and I'm not going to hand my niece over to a stranger with no concept of how to take care of her!" said Sophie hotly, blindly saying the only thing she could think of to make this man leave.

"It doesn't appear you're much of an expert yourself!" retorted Samson, gesturing to Sophie's rather inept holding of Alana. "And she should be with her father."

"I would like you to leave," Sophie said, resolutely.

Samson glanced from Sophie to Alana, debating what to do. He glared at Sophie. "Fine, I'll go, but I'll be in touch soon," he said ominously before turning and going back through the hallway and out of the flat.

She kicked the door closed after him as both her hands were taken up with her niece and the bottle of formula., Her heart thumping in her chest, Sophie carried Alana into the sitting room and peeped around the drawn curtains to check on the street outside. Samson stood, staring thoughtfully at the house for a moment, before shaking his head and walking away. Sophie rubbed her forehead, it was beginning to ache, and looked down at her niece, who was seemingly unaware of all the drama unfolding around her and focused solely on drinking her bottle of milk.

It seemed to Sophie that just as her situation couldn't get any more complicated, this man's arrival messed things up even more. Samson, even if he was Alana's father, meant nothing to her niece. It seemed he couldn't pick his own daughter out of a line-up. A tiny voice in her head kept stubbornly pointing out that she was also an extremely new addition to Alana's world, but she ignored it: Natasha had been her sister, and Alana was all Sophie had left of her; there was no way she was going to give her niece up without a fight.

Sophie sunk down into an old armchair, already mentally exhausted by what had gone on. It seemed incredibly likely Samson was Alana's father. As far as she could see, her best hope was that being the surf bum he clearly was, he'd swiftly lose interest in the idea of having a child. He couldn't exactly have been very reliable before, otherwise he'd already be playing some part in Alana's life. The more she thought about it, the more certain she became that whatever feelings of paternal responsibility he was currently experiencing would swiftly pass.

Sophie relaxed a little and became absorbed in watching her tiny niece guzzling down the milk. She was so beautiful. Alana finished and pushed away her bottle before letting out a huge burp. "Pardon you," said Sophie, smiling.

She was contemplating attempting to get up and make herself a cup of coffee when the doorbell rang again. Sophie felt her heart begin to beat faster. Was this Samson back? Was he going to force her to hand over Alana to him immediately? Should she ignore the door? The knocking that followed the ringing indicated he was unlikely to give up. She'd have to face him and stand her ground.

Sophie carried Alana back through to the hallway and reopened the front door, only to find herself facing not Samson, but a small, smartly dressed woman. She appeared in her fifties, with a greying bob, and held a folder in her hands.

"Hello, can I help you?" Sophie asked.

"Good morning, my name's Yvonne, I'm from Social Services. I'm here to check in on Alana. Is this her?" the woman said, smiling, and holding out her hand to the baby, who eyed this newcomer suspiciously.

Sophie felt a moment of panic. What had the woman from Rodney Street gone and said?

"Yes, this is Alana. I'm Sophie, her aunt."

"I see. May I come in for a little chat?"

"Of course, come through," said Sophie, nervously. "Sorry I'm not dressed yet, we slept in."

Sophie led the social worker into the small living room, cringing at the mess, the unvacuumed carpet, and old mugs lying about the place, and seeing the situation through Yvonne's eyes.

"I'm sorry about the state of the place . . . Would you like a cup of tea?"

"I'm fine, thank you," said Yvonne, pleasantly. "May I sit down?"

"Please!"

Yvonne perched on the edge of the small, lumpy sofa, and Sophie resumed her earlier position in the armchair.

"This is a routine visit in the circumstances, nothing for you to worry yourself about. My department was contacted this morning about your sister when her records showed she had a child. The hospital said Natasha had a sister and they thought you'd be caring for the baby. Without an address for you, this seemed the obvious place to check first. May I offer my condolences? Her passing must have been a terrible shock."

"Thank you. It was." Sophie felt some relief at this opening.

"Of course, you won't have had a chance to think long term about Alana," Yvonne continued. "I understand there's no dad in the picture though? It says 'father unknown' on her records?"

"Yes . . . Alana doesn't know her father," answered Sophie, not wanting to go into the details of Samson's earlier visit.

"So, you're her guardian at the moment then?"

Sophie nodded her reply.

"Is there anyone to help you?"

"No. We're fine as we are. I can manage."

"I would be able to find a place in foster care for her if it's needed? Even if it's just while you get yourself together . . ." Yvonne offered.

"No!" said Sophie, quickly. "That won't be necessary."

"So you're happy to care for her long term?"

"Absolutely," Sophie said, firmly.

"And do you have children yourself?"

"No . . ." admitted Sophie.

"Don't worry," said Yvonne, kindly. "Would it be all right if I left my phone number with you, and took down a number for you? Any problems or queries, give me a call straight away, any time."

"Sure," Sophie replied, breathing a sigh of relief, and accepting the contact details Yvonne offered. She wrote her mobile number down.

"I'll need to check in every now and again to see how you two are doing. Maybe we could meet in about a week to talk about how you'd like to proceed with making your guardianship official? You live locally?"

"No, in London."

"Oh. So you'll be going back there?"

"I don't know, I suppose so . . . I haven't thought . . ."

"OK. What's your actual address?" Yvonne noted it down in her folder. A few more questions followed about Sophie and her life, and the pen scribbled away.

"Well, let me know if there's anything I can do to help," said Yvonne finally, standing up to leave.

"Thank you, I will," said Sophie, showing her to the front door.

"Good luck to you both," said Yvonne.

Sophie gratefully shut the door. Yvonne had seemed nice and supportive, but she'd been so worried Alana would start screaming, or that Yvonne would spot she was doing something completely wrong with the baby and would insist she wasn't capable of being her niece's guardian, she'd been on tenterhooks for the whole conversation. She hadn't even noticed that Alana had contentedly fallen asleep in her arms. Sophie quickly carried her niece to her cot and placed her gently in it, resolved to at least have a quick shower and get dressed before the doorbell rang again.

What a start to looking after Alana. Surely things could only improve from now on.

CHAPTER 3

Samson's dig about how she'd seemed like she had no idea what she was doing with her niece spurred Sophie on: she needed to learn how to care for Alana, and quickly. She was solely in charge of this little human being, and there was no room for mistakes. But, strangely, the burden of this expectation didn't weigh heavy on her. As tired and grieving as she was, there was nothing as important as the baby in her arms. How her life had changed so dramatically in less than twenty-four hours, and how strangely worthless Sophie's previous existence seemed when compared to her niece holding her hand while she was feeding. Nothing else was anywhere near as important as Alana.

Her natural tendency to organise kicked in. She began researching baby care on her mobile phone, trying to get an idea of what you do with an infant all day, what on earth you feed them, and generally, how to keep a small, delicate human being alive. How did we manage before the internet to tell us what to do? she thought.

While Alana sat on a playmat in the middle of the sitting room floor with some toys Sophie found lying around, Sophie wrote out a feeding and sleep schedule for her and a basic meal plan for over the next couple of days.

There wasn't much food in the house, and not a huge amount of nappies and formula, so Sophie figured she'd need to face the supermarket with her niece soon. She'd make a list of what was needed and the fresh air would do her good. She felt better and a little more in control of the situation until she tried to put Alana down for a nap after her lunch. Alana didn't approve of this part of her aunt's programme. As soon as Sophie placed her down in her cot, on her back as all the websites she'd visited advised, her niece's beautiful little rosebud mouth opened to an extent Sophie didn't believe possible and let out an absolutely ear-splitting scream. Anyone listening would think the poor child was being murdered. Sophie scooped her up again immediately. Maybe this wasn't going to be as straightforward as the schedule suggested, Sophie thought to herself as she kissed her still snuffling niece on the forehead.

* * *

A week later, and Sophie was still living in Natasha's flat and trying to decide what to do for the future. Work had been very understanding when she'd called and explained what had happened to her sister, but she hadn't told them about Alana. They'd offered her some leave, and she'd added some holiday she was owed, so had two weeks to properly figure out what to do. It was the longest time she'd had off work since getting her first full-time job after university.

She knew she couldn't stay in her sister's home for ever: it was small and much too far for her to commute to work for a start, and it was a council flat — she'd already been contacted about when she had to hand back the keys. But it was where Alana knew and where Natasha's belongings were. There was no one but Sophie to sort through it all and decide what to keep for Alana, and no one else to arrange Natasha's funeral.

Yvonne, the social worker, had been in touch and visited again. She seemed satisfied with how things were going.

She'd advised Sophie on the first steps for her to gain at least temporary official guardianship of Alana, and Sophie had a solicitor on the case.

"I'll be away for the next couple of weeks, but you can leave a message with my department and someone will get back to you if it's urgent," Yvonne had said at the end of the visit.

Sophie got through each day by following the routine she'd drawn up for Alana, throwing herself into caring for her niece and learning everything she could about bringing up a child. Disjointed from 'real', regular life, the two of them were in a little bubble together.

Alana was surprisingly good company and Sophie found she didn't feel as alone as she so often had living by herself in London. Even if the baby wasn't the greatest conversationalist.

Having responsibility for her niece gave meaning to Sophie's day but also allowed her to cry and grieve when she needed to.

She was gradually gaining in confidence, exploring what Alana wanted and needed, but still had to steel herself every time they ventured outside. Caring for a baby out of the home and among other people was far trickier, she found, than staying inside. When she was out, she was constantly worried everyone would see her for the fraud she was, and think she wasn't the best person to care for her niece.

Finally, though, she decided they needed to go somewhere other than the supermarket. Sophie wasn't ready to brave the baby story-time at the library she'd seen advertised, but it was a lovely day and Natasha's flat didn't have a garden. The sky was a deep blue, smudged with only the occasional fluffiest of white cloud; the light breeze took the edge flawlessly off the summer heat and brought the fresh smell of the sea faintly into the building; in short, it was perfection. A walk after Alana's 11 a.m. bottle would be a nice change and would be good for her niece.

Sophie packed anything they might need for their outing while Alana had her nap; even after only a week, she'd discovered it was always better to be overprepared when it came to dealing with babies.

They headed off towards Brighton's city centre, which she had never seen before. Sophie set them a mission of finding a sunhat for Alana. Their pace was painfully slow as she kept stopping every couple of minutes to check Alana was all right and wishing she had a backwards-facing buggy.

They walked along the Lanes. Sophie worried about the buggy on the cobblestones, but Alana didn't seem to mind. They stopped every now and then to check out things that caught Sophie's eye in the shop windows. She hoped she'd have time to explore more while she was in Brighton.

Her phone guided her to the huge Primark on Western Road where she found a cute pink hat for Alana along with some sunglasses and a summer dress. The sunglasses were promptly thrown on the floor the second they exited the store, but Sophie consoled herself that Alana had looked very sweet in them for the twenty seconds she'd had them on.

They returned home from their thirty-minute walk without any mishap, though Sophie wished her confidence had been up to stopping for a hot drink; the smells from the coffee shops they passed had been very enticing and she was missing her regular skinny latte treat.

Her elation was spoilt when she opened the front door to Natasha's flat and found a handwritten note on the mat. From Samson. It was scribbled in the margin of a torn-up political pamphlet, 'Came to visit Alana. Call me. Samson.' It was blunt. He'd given a mobile number.

Sophie's first thought was to screw the whole thing up and throw it in the bin, but some part of her reconsidered, and she shoved it in the drawer by the fridge along with the piles of council tax demands and random keys and closed it firmly away. She had enough to deal with now, but knew she wouldn't be able to ignore Samson for ever — and shouldn't. That wouldn't be fair to Alana or him — but he couldn't take precedence at the moment.

Sophie began to prepare some lunch, keeping one eye on Alana playing in the all-singing, all-dancing walker Sophie had had delivered for her. The noise was enough to drive any normal adult crazy after a few minutes, but her niece loved it, so Sophie tried to last as long as she could with Alana banging away.

Her attention wasn't really focused on either the baby or the scrambled egg and toast she was making; it was on the pile of papers on the counter next to her. Or rather on trying to pretend it didn't exist. They'd sat there since yesterday when she'd tried to deal with them all, but had broken down in tears. The post-mortem results had returned from the coroner. Her sister's body was with the undertaker. And the papers represented all that was left to organise to tie up Natasha's too short life.

Sophie received at least some solace from the post-mortem results: Natasha hadn't been drunk the night she died. Though Sophie now felt terribly guilty that because of Natasha's past, she'd assumed alcohol had played a major part in what had happened. It turned out Natasha had swerved suddenly, presumably to avoid something. Her death had been a terrible accident.

Nothing could be said to 'console' about any of it, but at least Natasha had crashed into the barrier: there was no one else involved, no one else injured, or, thank goodness, killed. Tears filled her eyes as Sophie glanced down at her niece; she was eternally thankful Alana hadn't been in the car.

After lunch, Sophie forced herself to return to arranging the funeral. Natasha didn't have any savings. Sophie had felt a little uncomfortable going through her sister's paperwork but Sophie would pay for the funeral and wake out of her own money. Most of the logistics had been sorted out, but the big problem was working out who to invite.

She hadn't seen Natasha for so long, and they hadn't been close for even longer. Sophie had no idea who her friends were. The only family she and her sister had were each other. She'd contacted a few old family friends, who'd expressed their condolences, but most wouldn't be attending the funeral. In order to get in touch with anyone else who might want the opportunity to say goodbye to Natasha, Sophie would have to go through Natasha's phone, she supposed, something she had a particular loathing to do. More than anything else, it felt like such an invasion of privacy. Not that that mattered now, but it felt so wrong, so intrusive. It was different from turning the phone on at the hospital to discover who'd been trying to get hold of her; this was delving into the most personal part of her sister's life, a life Sophie hadn't been part of.

Retrieving the mobile from the hospital bag it had remained in, she got it charging by the side of the bed and busied herself with a few admin matters for the funeral, before it was time to settle Alana for her afternoon nap. Finally, and without any more excuses, she sat in the silence of the flat and turned the phone on.

Sophie worked through the text messages first, noting anyone Natasha had been in touch with recently, but there weren't many, barely a handful of numbers.

Made and missed calls resulted in a similar meagre haul, and one of those contacts was clearly identifiable as the blue-haired woman from Rodney Street. She couldn't help noticing the only record of Samson was a few calls from him from the night and morning after the accident.

The device must have been fairly new, and presumably Natasha hadn't ported her number from a previous phone, because the messages only went back about six months or so.

She moved onto WhatsApp and Facebook Messenger. Ah, bingo! There were many more messages here. She worked through them all methodically, not wanting to miss anyone meaningful or important, but mindful to read no more than she absolutely had to: she didn't want to accidentally contact a random stranger who Natasha had bought baby clothes from on Facebook Marketplace or something. Her list grew slowly.

Afterwards, there didn't seem to be any other app immediately obvious on the phone for communication, so she decided to bite the bullet and start calling people while Alana was still sleeping.

By the final call, Sophie was exhausted. It was hard and very strange breaking the news of her sister's death to strangers over the telephone. It felt far too personal and raw for her to be sharing with people she didn't know. But she was glad she'd done it and felt relieved the ordeal was over. A few people had thankfully offered to pass the word around Natasha's circle, so she needn't worry she'd missed anyone. And this way she didn't have to decide whether or not to contact the angry blue-haired lady: either she was close enough that she'd hear and could make her own decision what to do, or she wasn't and it wouldn't matter.

It hadn't been all bad: it had been good to speak with others who knew Natasha, who she could share her grief with. The whole experience left her feeling less alone in her sadness.

It wasn't all quite done though, was it? Samson's note was haunting her. He should be told about the funeral. He'd obviously had a relationship of sorts with her sister, and it *might* be that he'd want to say goodbye.

With a sigh, and genuinely not knowing whether or not she was doing the right thing, she took Samson's note out of the drawer and picked up her own mobile to call him, but chickened out at the last minute. She was completely wrung out and couldn't deal with another confrontation with him today. At that moment she heard Alana waking up in the next room which finalised her decision. She'd have to leave speaking to him for now; she could hardly call him with Alana crying in the background.

* * *

The evening before Natasha's funeral, Sophie put Alana into her cot after her bath, stories and bottle. They were both getting used to their routine and it was Sophie's favourite part of the day. She turned on the night light by the side of the cot and kissed her niece good night, longing to stay in there with her and watch her go to sleep, but knowing Alana would think it was definitely still playtime if she hung around. She'd come and check on her in a while.

Sophie walked wearily into the kitchen, and flicked on the kettle, wishing she had some wine in instead so she could drown her sorrows at least a little. Her mind was going over the arrangements for the following day, especially the babysitter from a very well-respected local agency who she'd booked to look after Alana, which was actually what she was most nervous about. She tidied the papers on the side and found Samson's note amongst them. Guilt flooded through her; he should know about the funeral. It wouldn't be right if she didn't tell him. If he decided not to come, that was his choice. But she didn't need to speak to him. She got out her mobile and typed out a text message giving the details for the next day and then sent it before she had a chance to change her mind.

* * *

Natasha's funeral was small, held in a crematorium suggested by the funeral director, which, not being a local, Sophie had never even driven past before. The service was short and non-religious, as Sophie guessed Natasha would have wanted. Sarah McLachlan's 'Angel' played as everyone filed out, Sophie remembered her sister liking it as a teenager.

Sophie consoled herself with the fact that everyone there seemed to have genuinely cared about Natasha. Everyone spoke about her affectionately and had a touching memory to share. The sad news had indeed been passed around as promised: surprisingly there were even several wreaths sent from various exotic places her sister had briefly lived in across the world, all with very thoughtful and heartfelt messages attached.

For the first time in her life Sophie was glad her parents were no longer with her. Burying their child was something no parent should ever have to go through.

It was only when the service was over, and people were making their way outside, that Sophie spotted Samson in the back row. He caught her eye and nodded and she managed to nod back before, thankfully, another one of Natasha's friends came over to give her condolences.

Sophie could feel Samson watching her as she moved around the wake she'd organised in a hotel meeting room close to the crematorium. She tried to make sure she spoke to everyone, thanking them for coming and finding out about their relationship with her sister.

The funeral itself had felt cathartic, like she was properly able to say goodbye to Natasha, but she found it hard to hold herself together afterwards. She was emotionally exhausted and wanted to be away from these people she didn't know, to stop having to be polite and make small talk. She wanted to be back with Alana and her vibrant, simplistic expression of life.

She suspected Samson was waiting until everyone had left before confronting her. She could see him out of the corner of her eye as she said goodbye to Natasha's friends. The final mourner left and Sophie had paid the bill at the reception when he strode over. She had no opportunity to slip away.

"Where's Alana?" he asked gruffly and without any preamble.

"She's with a babysitter. I didn't think a funeral was the best place to bring a baby."

Samson's face softened and Sophie felt guilty for not admitting this was only part of why she hadn't brought Alana to her mother's funeral. The whole truth was Sophie still didn't feel confident enough to handle Alana while surrounded by Natasha's super cool, world traveller, hippy friends, and also wanted to be able to mourn her sister without having to worry about naps, bottles and full nappies.

"Thank you for letting me know about today," Samson said in a much gentler tone, "I'm glad I was able to come."

He gave a cheerless smile and, for a split second, Sophie was glad he'd come as well, and said, "I'm sorry I didn't reply to your note properly. There's been a lot to deal with, a lot of readjustment and organising today . . ."

"I understand that, and I'm sorry for your loss. But I have to see my daughter," Samson said kindly, though with definite resolve.

"I know . . ." began Sophie.

"When can I see her?"

Sophie sighed. She didn't want to be dealing with this right now. She wanted to go home to Alana and her bedtime routine. She needed to hold Alana to her, to smell her hair after her bath, and cover her tummy with kisses.

"Things got a little . . . away from us, when I came round. Let's try to take a step back. I know you said you were worried about me telling the truth, whether I am Alana's father. Well . . ." He handed her a folded piece of paper. She opened it apprehensively; it was Alana's birth certificate, naming Natasha as her mother and with a blank space for her father's details.

"When Natasha told me about Alana, she wanted me to see that the um . . . dates added up and they match with when we were together," he said.

Sophie's first thought was that she knew Alana's birthday now — she'd been born on 1 December. This pleasure was rapidly followed though by the necessary acknowledgement of Samson's right to see Alana. Natasha clearly thought he was the father and there was no denying the physical resemblance. Yes, Sophie was Alana's only maternal blood relative, but as her father, presumably Samson would be well within his rights to demand regular access to Alana, if not full parental authority. Dread filled Sophie's stomach as she tried desperately to figure out the best way to deal with the situation. He wasn't actually named on the certificate, was he? All she could think was she should go along with what he wanted for now and then get legal advice if she became worried he wanted to take Alana from her permanently.

"What about tomorrow?" Samson pushed.

"Sure," Sophie agreed, mainly so she could remove herself from the situation as quickly as possible and have some time to work out exactly how she wanted to play things to protect herself and Alana. Then she remembered she had plans. "But it'll need to be early. I need to leave by eleven for a meeting in London."

"That's not a problem. Eight on the beach?"

"OK."

"Come by my campervan. It'll be parked in the Madeira Drive car park, not far from the pier, as close to the beach as I can get it. It's blue. You really can't miss it."

"I'll see you there," said Sophie, gratefully turning to go and thinking how right her first impressions of Samson had been. He must be in his early thirties at least, and living in a campervan on the beach! Not exactly a stable father figure for her niece, but absolutely typical of the sort of man her sister would go for, and, from Sophie's past experience of Natasha's boyfriends, would be completely unreliable and untrustworthy. She'd never been able to understand what her sister saw in them. Sure, they were all ridiculously handsome, and Natasha had been drawn to someone wild and unpredictable like herself, but more than that, they were all self-destructive. Did she want to redeem them? And validate herself? Or was it something similarly self-destructive? Did she feel worthless and sought to punish herself? Who knew? Certainly not Natasha, Sophie had always thought.

Sophie resented having to deal with such characters. She had enough going on in her life at the moment without adding a surfer bum into it. But he was Alana's father, and she couldn't keep the two of them apart, even if she believed it was in her niece's best interests.

CHAPTER 4

The next morning was the first time Sophie had had to get herself and Alana ready to go out early, and it was certainly a learning experience. It seemed the more she tried to hurry her niece, the more determined the little girl became to take her sweet time. How slowly was it possible to drink a bottle of milk? Each leaden minute crawled by.

Somehow Sophie had Alana ready to leave only fifteen minutes after she'd planned to, but catching sight of herself in the hallway mirror as she carried the baby out to the car, made her gasp. She was a total state. She'd managed a super-fast shower but hadn't had time to put any make-up on, let alone properly brush her hair. She'd dragged on some clothes she'd found on the floor by the side of the bed.

She had to sort herself out before she left, there was no way she could turn up to see Samson like that; he'd think she wasn't fit to look after herself, let alone Alana. And as slowly as things were moving today, she might not have time to pop back and freshen up as planned before heading off to London. She turned around and marched back to her bedroom determinedly. She popped her niece on the floor with some toys, and much to Alana's amusement, gave her hair a quick blast with the hairdryer. Sophie smoothed out her skin with some tinted moisturiser and put on some of her old 'work' clothes that she'd picked up from her own flat when she'd done a quick trip there to grab essentials, including her outfit for the funeral. Looking smart and professional would mean she would be taken seriously and her suggestions considered fairly. And, as handsome as he was unsuitable, she needed to concentrate on the fact that the meeting she was having at her offices today was actually the big event, not dropping by to see Samson at his campervan. She could hardly attend a business meeting in jeans and a T-shirt with apple puree down it.

Alana acquiesced, with only minimal squeaking, to being put in the super-duper top of the range car seat Sophie had bought and had fitted for her, and they got on their way, with Sophie doing her very best to smooth her justifiably frazzled nerves.

Thankfully they found a parking space immediately, and Samson's van was easy to spot across the car park. It wasn't worth getting the buggy out, and it would be useless if they moved on to the stony beach, so Sophie left it in the boot and, picking her niece up, marched as quickly as she could in her work heels towards the blue campervan, cursing how warm the day already was. She would swear she could feel the small amount of make-up she'd put on sliding down her face.

They reached the campervan and, a now rather sweaty Sophie, knocked on the door and waited. There was no reply. She knocked again. Once more, there was no reply. Furious at her time being wasted, and at herself for how disappointed she was, Sophie turned and was stomping off back to her car, when she heard her name called. She glanced over her shoulder and spotted Samson jogging up the beach.

He wore a wetsuit rolled down to his waist, his chest bare and dripping wet. He dried his blond hair with a towel as he came towards them. Trotting alongside him was some sort of giant Irish wolfhound. It was possibly the biggest dog Sophie had ever seen. Its legs seemed to go in all directions at once as it picked up its pace and began to hurtle towards her, its grey fur pulled backwards by his speed. It bounded ahead of Samson and shook itself all over Sophie, who had turned away to protect Alana from the dog and was clutching the baby tightly to her. The animal gave a deep woof, making Sophie jump. Alana squealed with delight and tried to get out of her aunt's arms to investigate.

"Hey," said Samson cheerfully, smiling at his daughter, and ignoring the dog, still sniffing around Sophie.

"Could you get that animal away from us?" asked Sophie, crossly. "He's soaked me and is scaring Alana!"

Samson lifted an eyebrow and seemed to be hiding a smile, but grabbed hold of the dog's collar without arguing. "Come on Mutt," he said affectionately and opened the door of the campervan. "Get in there for a bit."

The dog gave Sophie a dejected look, clearly blaming her for his dismissal. With a sigh, he lumbered into the van, and Samson closed the door.

"Thank you," said Sophie stiffly.

"No problem. I'm sorry he shook on you and upset Alana."

Sophie focused awkwardly on brushing down her clothes.

"I'll dry soon and Alana's fine," she conceded. "I've always been nervous around dogs."

"You don't need to worry about Mutt, he's a gentle giant. I found him abandoned on the beach when he was a puppy. He wouldn't hurt a fly."

"He's very big," Sophie said, "And Alana's so small."

"Trust me," Samson said gently. "Come inside and we can introduce them properly while I make a cup of tea. Can I give Alana a cuddle?"

Sophie handed the baby over to her father's outstretched arms.

As Samson then proceeded to carry Alana into his campervan, Sophie didn't have much choice but to follow.

The inside of the van was much tidier than Sophie had expected. There didn't seem to be very much in there, the only real 'stuff' was a shelf packed full of rather dog-eared books. Samson hung up his towel on a hook behind the door, and while Mutt greeted him enthusiastically, like they'd been apart for years, Sophie tried awkwardly to move out of the way in the tiny space so as not to be anywhere near his naked chest.

"Would you like tea or coffee?" asked Samson as he carefully balanced Alana on his hip. She could tell he was being extremely cautious as he poured water from a bottle into a camping kettle which he then placed on the little hob on the top of his kitchen counter. Despite his height, he only had to stoop ever so slightly. She didn't know what to do with herself: most of the space inside the van was taken up by people and dog, and the only place to sit was on the bed, which seemed far too intimate.

"Tea would be great, thanks."

"How do you take it?"

"Milk, no sugar please," she replied. "Can I do anything?" Mutt was now sniffing around her again and she eyed him suspiciously. She wanted nothing more than to be out of this very uncomfortable situation. Her cheeks felt flushed, she was sweating, and terribly self-conscious.

"Why don't you take Alana back outside and I'll bring the teas in a minute?" suggested Samson.

Sophie breathed a sigh of relief at the thought of removing herself from this enclosed space. Samson's muscular chest had a drop of water slowly working its way down it. She retrieved Alana as quickly as she could and carried her outside, relishing the cooling fresh air on her face. She closed the door firmly on Mutt — if Samson wanted his huge dog to join them that was his choice, but she certainly wasn't going to be left in charge of him.

Thankfully when Samson emerged from the campervan a few minutes later, he had donned a shirt, though not one which covered his thick, rippling upper arms, Sophie couldn't help observing. Mutt dutifully joined his master.

"Here you go," Samson said, giving Sophie a large, steaming mug. "Would you like me to hold her for you?"

"Sure." Sophie handed Alana back over. So far the whole encounter had felt like a bizarre, and rather uncomfortable, game of pass the baby parcel.

"Grab a perch," Samson suggested, indicating the step leading up to the campervan's door before sitting down there himself.

"I'm fine standing," said Sophie, not wanting to be stuck sitting in such close proximity to him now she'd managed to make her escape from the cramped confines of the van.

She ventured a sip from her tea and grimaced as it burnt her tongue.

"Bit hot?" commented Samson, who'd placed his drink by his feet so he'd have both hands free to hold Alana who was investigating his hair, much to his obvious delight. He was clearly completely charmed by his daughter.

Sophie nodded. She just wanted to down her damn drink and have this stupid 'playdate' over with so she could leave and get on with her day. How long did they need to stay? Would an hour be enough?

That thought brought back the realisation that she had her meeting to go to and her stomach gave a flip. Her career had been her life for so long, she wasn't used to not being able to give one hundred per cent to it, and she didn't think her boss would react well to her asking if she could be home-based, especially as she'd already been away from the office for almost two weeks.

There followed a few moments of uncomfortable silence. Sophie glanced around at the beach and the sky, anywhere but at Samson. Eventually, Samson asked, "So where is it you need to get off to today?"

"I've got a meeting at my offices in London. I had the last couple of weeks off to deal with everything, but need to speak to them about going back."

"So, you live in London?"

"Yes, I've got a place in South Norwood. I was only staying in Natasha's flat while I sorted out the funeral and all her stuff."

"Where do you work?"

"I'm an accountant. I work for a large firm in the centre of London."

"Sounds like long hours," commented Samson.

"They can be," Sophie answered cautiously.

"I hope you don't mind me asking, but how are you going to manage that? You're young, live by yourself, have no experience of children and no support network as far as I can tell. How do you think you're going to look after Alana on your own and work?" Samson asked.

"There are plenty of single mothers who cope perfectly well," replied Sophie quickly.

"Of course there are, but it's not an easy route to go down, and many have help from family. What exactly do you know about caring for a baby?"

"At least as much as you, I imagine," Sophie retorted.

"So, you've made plans?"

"Nothing concrete," she admitted. "I guess I'll use daycare or something."

"Won't that take a while to sort out?"

"I don't know . . . maybe," she said lamely.

"You don't have a plan at all, do you?"

"I've only been her guardian for a couple of weeks — I think I'm doing pretty well actually!"

"Well she can't go into full-time daycare, she's tiny and has just lost her mother," stated Samson, adamantly.

Sophie's hackles rose. She agreed completely, it was too soon after Natasha's death for Alana to be away from her for long hours — as young as she was she'd be distressed by the change, the upset — but she resented Samson saying it. It was she who'd been looking after Alana, her life which had been turned upside down.

"I know, that's why I'm having the meeting today so I can work out how to arrange things," Sophie said, struggling to keep her temper in check, desperately not wanting another acrimonious parting between them.

"Who's going to have Alana for you while you're in your meeting?" Samson asked, pleasantly enough, but Sophie took his questioning as checking up on how she was managing things with Alana.

"She's coming with me," Sophie answered shortly.

"That's not very professional," Samson pointed out. Annoyingly, he was right, and she'd been worrying about it. Her office wasn't exactly baby-friendly and she wanted to appear as competent as ever, simply needing to adjust her working hours and be home-based as much as possible. What would she do if Alana had a meltdown because she wasn't allowed to grab at some computer wires or something?

"Well, there's not a lot I can do. I don't have anyone to babysit," she retorted, but regretted it instantly.

"I'll do it," Samson said, with an easy shrug.

"Oh . . . um . . . thank you," Sophie managed to stutter, frantically searching her mind for a good excuse to get out of leaving Alana in a campervan with a huge dog and a lay-about beach bum. "But, well, Alana doesn't know you and . . ."

Her argument might have been somewhat more convincing if Alana didn't seem so completely content being held by her father. She blushed and tried a different tack, "And there's your dog . . ."

Alana had to choose this moment to grab hold of Mutt's ear. Sophie jumped up to save her niece from being savaged. Mutt was completely unperturbed by the baby's attention and gave her a friendly lick in return before calmly slipping under the van to lie in the shade.

"Mutt will be fine, but I promise I won't leave them alone together," Samson conceded. Sensing Sophie still wasn't convinced, he said, "I am her father."

There was nothing Sophie could say to counter that. She knew it would be helpful not to have Alana in the office, and Samson was good with her and certainly seemed far more competent than she'd previously thought. It wasn't like she could stop Alana's father from having her for a few hours.

"All right then, thank you," she said as graciously as she could manage. "I should be back by three at the latest."

"That's fine, take your time — there's no hurry. We'll be fine," Samson said, bouncing a giggling and delighted Alana on his knee.

"Her next bottle is due at eleven, and then she'll need a nap. She'll sleep in her buggy, which is in my car, as long as you push her around a bit to get her off," Sophie fussed. "And you mustn't let her take off her hat in the sun, in fact, keep her out of the sun, especially in the middle of the day. Her sunblock needs to be applied every hour."

"Why does she need sunblock?" interrupted Samson, trying to hide his grin. "She's not supposed to go in the sun."

Sophie glared at him.

"Fine," he agreed, "I'll remember the sunblock."

"There's a jar of food in her bag for her lunch, but make her take it slowly or she'll be sick . . ."

"We'll be fine," Samson said reassuringly. "I have your mobile number. If there's any problem, I'll call straight away."

Sophie had to concede it made much more sense for Alana to stay with Samson rather than be strapped in her seat to and from London and somehow entertained during her meeting.

They walked back to Sophie's car, Sophie carrying Alana, so Samson could retrieve the buggy and Alana's bag full of supplies from the boot. She gave Alana a kiss and cuddle goodbye and was only a little put out that her niece was clearly more interested in Mutt than she was in her aunt. She didn't want the baby to be upset of course, but a little recognition that she was being left with someone who was almost a stranger would have been nice.

Once Sophie began driving, and Samson and Alana were well out of sight, she resolved to concentrate on work. She would spend the journey going over in her mind what she wanted to say and what she felt the different options were, and hope that her boss decided she was worth making exceptions for.

* * *

42

Sophie returned to the beach five hours later. It hadn't taken long for her boss to tell her, in roundabout terms, that if she wanted to stay with the company, she'd have to continue her full-time hours working from their offices.

As Sophie drove back, she contemplated going to HR, making a fuss, fighting her case and quickly ruled it out — she couldn't give it the headspace right now. She thought she'd be more upset than she was at the realisation she couldn't continue working for them. Her job had been everything to her; she loved being an accountant. The meticulous nature of her profession suited her, and she'd spent several years painstakingly working her way up through the ranks. Sometimes she'd worked twelve- or fourteen-hour days, had conference calls with international clients at all manner of strange times. She simply wasn't prepared to do that to Alana, not after she'd only just lost her mother. Sophie's priorities had changed dramatically in the last couple of weeks.

But she wasn't under any illusions that the path ahead would be trouble-free. The most immediate problem was how could she afford to live without her job? She could work freelance part-time from home, but it would take a while to set up. She wouldn't be able to afford her mortgage for long without any income coming in.

She parked her car in the same car park as earlier, though she struggled to find a space now the day was warmer and the beach busier, and walked over to the campervan. It was closed up, but continuing down onto the rocks, and scanning around her, she quickly spied Alana and Samson by the edge of the water, and she wandered down to them.

Samson was crouched down with Alana in his arms, letting her kick her feet in the waves. Alana was giving little shrieks of happy laughter. Sophie almost didn't join them as they were having so much fun together. She was considering heading back up the beach to get a coffee and give them some more time, when Samson turned around, waved and pointed her out to Alana.

When they reached each other, Sophie was thrilled that Alana held out her arms to have a cuddle with her aunt. Samson handed her over straight away, saying, "I know she's in the sun, but it was only for a few minutes and she's got her hat and sun cream on."

"Don't worry," said Sophie. "It looks like she's had a wonderful time." She couldn't help doing a surreptitious check to make sure none of Alana's skin was turning pink. It was fine.

"She didn't sleep for ages, but she ate all her lunch," Samson said. "How did your meeting go?"

"Not great," Sophie admitted. "They weren't happy for me to work from home or go part-time. I can kind of understand why."

"What are you going to do?"

"I don't want to go down the legal route — it's too much right now. I told my boss I'd have to leave. So I have. I typed out my resignation letter in my office and handed it in straight away. I had a load of holiday still left over, and they were happy for me to use it to see out my notice period."

"Wow, are you OK with that?"

"I think so. My plan, as far as I have one, is to become self-employed and work from home. I've got some contacts, but it'll take a little while to get up and running properly."

"So are you going to stay living in Natasha's place?"

"I can't, it's owned by the council. I've got to have it all cleared out in a couple of weeks. I guess I'll go back to my flat in London, but I'm going to have to think about selling up and moving somewhere cheaper."

"Well . . . You could rent it out and move in with me," said Samson simply.

"What?"

He shrugged. "I want to get to know Alana better. That's the most important thing to me right now, and it'll be a lot trickier over a longer distance. And I have plenty of space. It could be a workable solution. If we can be civil with each other for more than a few hours," he joked, smiling to remove any sting.

Sophie couldn't stop herself glancing incredulously at the campervan. She didn't want to be rude to the man, especially given the generosity of his offer, but 'plenty of space'? Really? What was he thinking?

Samson followed her gaze and burst out laughing. "This isn't my house! This is where I store my surf stuff. I stay in it sometimes if I want to catch the waves early, like this morning."

"Where do you live then?"

"In a house. Like a regular person." He laughed.

Sophie blushed, embarrassed her presumption had been so caught out.

"But I don't know you. I can't move in with you," she said.

"I can't see another way for you to be able to set up a business, and for Alana not to be in childcare," Samson said bluntly. "I'm freelance too — I'm an architect. I work a lot from home, and can usually shift what hours I'm working around so I can have her when you're busy. It doesn't have to be a permanent solution. We could give it a trial for a couple of weeks and see how things go."

Sophie was very uncertain. She was thrown first of all by the thought of Samson being an architect and living in a house. She was needing to swiftly rework her opinion of him, having got him completely wrong.

It would make sense financially to move into Samson's home she supposed, and having someone to help with Alana would make a huge difference, especially as she was just starting out as a freelancer. And it would mean both she and Samson would get to be with Alana which, for the time being at least, would ease her worries about him deciding he wanted sole custody of her niece. But she couldn't move into a stranger's house!

Sensing it would do no good to force the issue and that Sophie needed time to mull things over, Samson suggested, "Think about it overnight and come round tomorrow to see the house."

Sophie found herself nodding her head in agreement. She supposed people did take in lodgers, didn't they? It wasn't completely out of the ordinary.

"I'll text you the address. Come at one, I'll make lunch."

"All right," Sophie said. It wouldn't do any harm to take a look. If it turned out to be a complete hovel, or he had a mad wife locked in the attic, she'd tell him the whole idea was a no go and move back to London, while planning to find somewhere cheaper to live as soon as possible.

But as logical as Sophie was trying to be about the whole situation, she couldn't ignore the fact that she was looking forward to seeing Samson's home. She was intrigued by how different he was turning out to be from what she'd originally assumed. And the thought of sleeping in the same house as him was definitely not as unappealing as she would have thought merely a few days ago. She found herself singing along happily to the radio on the short drive back to Natasha's flat, not acting at all like someone who'd just had to give up her job and had no concrete plans for what she was going to do to earn a living or even where she was going to live. In fact, she was acting very unlike herself indeed.

CHAPTER 5

Sophie stood outside the smart, dark green door of the attractive semi-detached Victorian house with her niece in her arms, wondering if she was making a seriously stupid decision coming to see Samson's home at all. Was the whole idea of her and Alana staying with him ridiculous? She didn't know herself at the moment, everything in her life had been thrown into disarray so suddenly. She felt she was stuck in some sort of survival mode; dealing with each new challenge and decision as well as she could as they arose, and doing her absolute best not to panic completely when it seemed that practically every day she was making huge, life-altering choices, with no real idea how they would pan out. At the forefront of her mind was always Alana. Every choice presented to her was dealt with according to how the repercussions of her decision would affect her niece.

She glanced around surreptitiously. It seemed like a good area. All the houses were a little back from the road, with small front gardens and wrought iron gates. The pavement was clean and tree-lined, and there was no traffic as it wasn't a through road.

She heard Mutt begin to bark as he presumably realised there were people outside, and was getting up the courage to knock on the front door when it was opened by Samson.

"You found it!" he said cheerfully, the huge grey dog by his side wagging its tail frantically at the sight of his new friends.

"Good directions," replied Sophie with a smile, though she eyed Mutt apprehensively as she handed Alana to her father.

"Come on through. Would you like a cuppa?"

"Sure, thanks," said Sophie, feeling awkward as she followed Samson inside and along his entrance hall.

"Your house is lovely," she commented honestly, taking in the original wooden bannisters on the staircase and all the other carefully restored Victorian features.

"Thanks, I've lived here for a couple of years. It was a bit of a mess when I bought it, but it's turned out pretty well I think."

That sounded like Samson had done the work himself; Sophie was impressed.

They passed a large dining room cum sitting room and went down a couple of steps. There was a small utility room off the hallway and then the kitchen. A scrubbed pine table was the focal point of the space and French doors led out onto a patio garden, with a black cast iron table and chairs shaded by an old, gnarly pear tree laden with growing fruits. It was a beautiful day and a soft breeze blew in through the doors, wafting with the delicious cooking smells filling the kitchen.

A fancy highchair was positioned in the corner of the room Sophie noticed. Samson saw her looking at it. "Do you think it'll be all right for her?" he asked. "It said it was for six months plus and easy to clean."

Sophie couldn't help thinking it was rather sweet that he was so concerned about getting exactly the right thing for Alana. "It's lovely," she said.

"I thought we'd eat outside if that's OK?"

"Great," she said. "Can I do anything to help?"

"Would you be able to rinse the salad for me? The salad spinner's next to the sink and the salad's in the bowl on the table."

Sophie set to work on the salad, noticing as she did, how comfortable Samson was with Alana. He seemed much more confident today holding her in one arm and chatting to her as he made the teas.

He handed Sophie her mug; she was surprisingly touched he'd remembered how she took it.

"Food will be about half an hour. Shall we go outside?"

The garden matched the house: beautifully designed and lovingly maintained. Old brick walls covered in honeysuckle enclosed the space, and beds filled with fragrant herbs and shrubs were dotted around the edges.

He'd set up a playpen filled with multi-coloured balls for Alana in the garden. He popped her in it, and the baby immediately began joyfully throwing the balls out, one by one, much to the adults' amusement. It could have been a clichéd scene out of a catalogue, she mused.

"I've been trying to learn about Alana's age group, and what she should be eating and playing with . . ." Samson began.

"Oh yes," said Sophie edgily, preparing herself for Samson telling her she was doing everything wrong with her niece and that he knew much better ways to do it, all based on the latest scientific research. Especially if she somehow let slip that her sole experience with Alana was no longer than his own. That was a fact she was determined to keep to herself.

"It's complicated, isn't it?" he continued, absentmindedly pushing back his hair with his hand. "I mean, there are so many contradictions. How do you know if you're doing anything right?"

Relieved, Sophie let out her held breath and blurted, "I know, it's impossible!"

"I just want one book or website which says exactly what to do!"

"I guess every baby's different . . ."

"That's what's so tricky! I spent half an hour staring at jars of baby food this morning trying to decide what to get Alana for lunch. I was going to cook her something from scratch, but it seems there are different levels of lumpiness and I had no idea what she was on."

"I'm sure whatever you got her will be fine," said Sophie smiling. She decided not to mention she'd brought a jar of baby food with her. It was in Alana's nappy bag because she hadn't been sure if he'd have anything in that was suitable.

"I ended up buying her the same as you'd sent with her yesterday," Samson admitted.

Sophie laughed.

"I like your garden," she commented.

"Thank you. It's not very child friendly at the moment, I'm afraid. I'm thinking of having the patio taken up and turf put down."

He's completely serious about rearranging his life for his daughter, Sophie pondered.

They talked about Alana for a while and then Samson served up lunch while Sophie brought the highchair outside and put her niece in. Samson handed the baby a rusk to chew on while they began eating. Sophie had never given Alana a rusk before because of the high sugar content but didn't say anything. She feared she was going to struggle 'sharing' her niece. In the last couple of weeks, she'd become very used to doing things her way with the little girl and not having anyone else to have to fall in with about her decisions.

The food was delicious: roasted chicken drumsticks in sticky ginger, honey, garlic, and soy sauce; coleslaw, new potatoes and a huge green salad. Sophie didn't often cook. When she was in London, she'd get back from work so late she was too tired to do more than pop something in the microwave or boil some pasta if she was feeling particularly energetic, and now, looking after Alana, and being so emotionally wrung out from dealing with Natasha's death, she'd continued pretty much the same habits. She couldn't remember the last time she'd had a meal made for her. She relished every bite and appreciated that Samson was trying hard to make a good impression in a very peculiar situation.

Alana began fussing and trying to reach for the food, so they put a few bits on her highchair tray for her to have a go at feeding herself with. Both Sophie and Samson did their best to appear unperturbed and nonchalant about it, but in reality, they were both petrified Alana was going to choke on a piece of potato and couldn't relax until she'd managed to throw it all off the tray and it had been hoovered up by a ready and waiting Mutt.

"Would you like a tour of the house?" Samson asked when they'd finished eating.

"Sure." Sophie got up and wiped Alana's sticky hands with some wet wipes from her bag. She was amazed by how peaceful it was, here in this little garden, enjoying the sunshine with this man she barely knew, and a baby whose existence she hadn't even been aware of three weeks ago, and who her whole life now revolved around.

"You've already seen the kitchen," Samson said, scooping Alana out of the highchair and leading Sophie back inside.

"Here's the den," he said, showing them a small sitting room at the back of the house. There was a flat-screen television on the wall and a cream two-seater sofa that looked very comfortable. A beautiful original open fireplace had been restored at the far end. Sophie could imagine relaxing in this room on a chilly winter's evening, the fire roaring, feet up on the coffee table, and a cup of hot chocolate in her hands.

Next came the utility room she'd spotted earlier, which led to a downstairs loo.

The larger sitting room cum dining room was also beautiful and had an entire wall of books along one side which Sophie was dying to have a snoop through: you could tell such a lot about a person by what books they read, and, in particular, which ones they chose to keep.

They went up the stairs. "This is my room," Samson pointed out as they passed an open doorway that Sophie couldn't help peeking through. It was tidy. She reserved judgement there because that could be part of trying to make a good impression. Maybe he was usually a complete slob.

Next to his room was a large bathroom and then Samson's office.

"This is your bedroom," said Samson to Alana when they came to the next door. "For when you come to stay," he added for Sophie's benefit, seeing uncertainty wash over her face.

Samson opened the door and stepped back to let Sophie enter first. The room had undoubtedly been decorated especially for Alana. The walls were painted pale blue with clouds and bird images stencilled on them. There was a wooden cot, a chest of drawers with changing mat, a selection of teddies, and even a set of bookshelves filled with children's books.

Alana reached out to the teddies and Samson put her on the soft, colourful rug in the centre of the floor and handed her the toys she pointed to, one at a time.

"How on earth did you get this ready so quickly?" Sophie asked, glancing around and taking it all in.

"I've been doing it since I found out about Alana, so she'd have somewhere to sleep when she came to visit."

"It's beautiful."

"Thanks. She seems to like it doesn't she?" said Samson, smiling at his daughter investigating the exciting new playthings.

Alana yawned. "It's time for her nap, isn't it?" Samson asked.

"Yeah . . ." She hadn't wanted to bring it up in case he was offended they were leaving too soon, but had also been worried Alana might start to get grouchy.

"Why don't we try her in her cot?"

"Sure," said Sophie, relieved. She found she didn't want to go yet. She and Samson had been getting along unexpectedly well and a large part of her was beginning to seriously consider his offer. It would certainly solve some of her most immediate problems. And aside from all that, she was enjoying having some adult company and being with someone as interested in talking about her niece as she was. "I'll change her nappy, and then we'll see how she takes to it."

"Do you mind if I do it?" Samson asked. "I've only changed one nappy in my life and that was yesterday."

"No problem. I'll pop downstairs and get the changing bag."

"I think I've got everything here," Samson said, pointing to a wicker basket by the end of the changing mat full of nappies and wet wipes.

"Great," Sophie said quietly. Samson was being fantastic and she was very much impressed, but part of her was suddenly feeling a little overwhelmed. She'd been caring for her niece for two weeks now and she still didn't feel she was anywhere near as organised as Samson was for Alana's needs. The nursery was perfect. In Natasha's flat, or in her own place in London come to think of it, there wasn't a spare room for Alana, and there was no space for all this baby stuff. That was all right for the moment as she was only tiny, but she'd definitely need a bedroom of her own at some point.

Everything here was so clean and new. Samson must have spent a fortune and worked like crazy to get it all ready in such a short space of time. She felt a little inadequate if she were being completely honest with herself.

Samson had picked Alana up and was putting her on the changing mat as she jabbered away happily to him in baby talk. Sophie tidied the teddies, feeling increasingly like a spare part, the contentment of a few minutes ago steadily evaporating.

"You're a bit stinky, aren't you?" Samson said, taking off the nappy. This was swiftly followed by, "Oh my Lord! Sophie, come and see this, is this normal? It's everywhere! It's up her back!"

"I'm afraid that's completely normal," Sophie said, laughing. "She's probably had a bit too much fruit."

"But it's everywhere!"

"Yep. Do you want a hand?" she asked.

"No," he said, determinedly. "I need to be able to do this by myself."

"Shall I go and get her a spare change of clothes?"

"I got her a couple of vests and some babygros. They're in the top drawer, could you pass me one of each?"

"Of course."

Sophie came over to the chest of drawers, Samson moved to the side as best as he could while holding Alana's legs in one hand, and attempting to clean her with wet wipes using the other. Alana herself found the whole situation rather amusing and was giggling uncontrollably to herself.

Sophie's arm touched Samson's for a second. She felt a tingle run right through her body and stepped back suddenly.

"Are you all right?" he asked, taking his gaze off his daughter for a second and locking eyes with Sophie.

"Yeah, sorry, I'm fine." Sophie, feeling flustered, handed him the clothes.

"Let me show you your room," Samson suggested, his attention now back on Alana, but still talking to Sophie. "That's where you'll sleep, if you decide you'd like to stay for a little while. It's next door, the guest bedroom."

"Sure." Sophie was glad to have the opportunity to put some space between her and Samson. She was feeling a bit freaked out by her body's reaction to touching his. At her age, was she seriously unable to control herself around a handsome man?

What could be her bedroom was as lovely as the rest of the house. Its wooden floorboards and white walls were gorgeous, and the large window with fitted Venetian blinds looked out over the garden. The double bed was made up with crisp white cotton linen, and the wardrobe and large chest of drawers would give her plenty of space for her clothes. She stood staring out of the window, contemplating the frankly bizarre situation she found herself in.

Was it ridiculous for her to be considering moving in here, even temporarily? She didn't know Samson, and she was grieving for her sister as well as learning how to be a parent to Alana, and now setting up her own business. She'd be crazy to add more change and readjustment into the situation. There was also the additional problem that the more time she spent with this man, the more she realised she was attracted to him. Anything happening between them would only serve to make her life even more complicated, and, from previous experience, any man her sister had been interested in would be an absolute nightmare as a boyfriend. Not that she wanted Samson to be her boyfriend! That would simply be too weird. How had her ordered life ended up like this?

On the other hand, taking herself out of the equation, there was no denying this house would be a wonderful home for Alana and had advantages for the baby which Sophie herself wouldn't be able to provide: her own bedroom and a garden to name just two. Sophie couldn't help comparing Samson's beautiful home with Natasha's flat. She trusted her sister had been a good mother, and she was sure her niece had never wanted for love, but her little flat was noisy and draughty, and Sophie and Alana weren't able to stay there long term. If she moved back to London she wasn't sure she could afford the mortgage payments on her flat if she didn't start getting work in quickly, and it also had no garden or bedroom for Alana.

Whether she liked it or not, Samson was serious about playing a large part in his daughter's life and was more than happy to go out of his way to do so. Sophie needed to be accommodating; both so that Alana had a relationship with her father, and because she didn't want to antagonise Samson while her guardianship of Alana was officially unresolved.

If she and her niece moved into Samson's house, even if it was only a temporary fix, both Samson and she would be able to see as much of Alana as they wanted. Plus she'd have the support of someone to help her with Alana while she set up her new business.

Samson came in and joined her. "I've put her in the cot and she seemed happy. Now we have to wait and see if she'll sleep in it."

Sophie smiled. "Fingers crossed."

"I set up the baby monitor I bought as well, which seems to be working fine." He held up the device in his hand.

"Great."

"Do you like the room?" Samson asked tentatively. "I know you'll need more time to decide about staying, that's fine. I'm not wanting to rush you."

Sophie took a moment to think: she knew very little about Samson, and this was the first time they'd been together without an undercurrent of animosity being very present in their conversation, but they did seem to be getting on better now. She had misjudged him, and she was able to see things from his point of view: of course he wanted to get to know his daughter properly. Perhaps this was a way to prevent a custody battle between her and Samson, or at least delay it until she was better prepared? It would certainly be convenient, and she wouldn't necessarily know a flatmate any better before moving in with them.

She decided to take a gamble, to stop stressing, and do what felt right at the moment. "I love it, and if the offer still stands, it would be brilliant if we could stay here. As a short-term thing, until I get myself sorted."

A huge grin spread across Samson's face. "That's brilliant! Stay for as long as you like!"

"I'd want to pay rent," Sophie said.

"Let's discuss that if you decide to stay for any length of time."

Sophie nodded. "That's sensible. When would you like us to move in?"

"When can you?"

"Today?" asked Sophie, laughing. Now she'd made the decision, there seemed no point in spending any more time than she needed to in Natasha's flat, which was so full of her sister's presence it made her feel morbid, plus the truth was she didn't feel safe there. The area was rowdy with plenty of pubs around the blocks of flats, and having drunks walk by the window after throwing out time wasn't pleasant at all. And renting out her own place would ease her financial situation significantly. "If you can watch Alana, I can pick up our stuff from Natasha's flat. It won't take me long."

"Of course, but are you sure you wouldn't like a hand?"

"Thank you for the offer, but I'll be fine. I can fit it all in the car. I'll get off now while she's sleeping if that's all right?" They hadn't heard a peep from the room next door; either they'd worn Alana out or she really loved her new cot.

* * *

A couple of hours later, and Sophie had returned with a car-load of stuff which Samson helped her to unpack. It was amazing how much she'd brought back with her. Alana's walker had taken up a fair bit of space by itself. Well, it would all need to have been taken from the flat soon anyway, so she saw it as doing part of the clearing out of Natasha's home early.

Sophie's own possessions only amounted to a couple of small suitcases at the moment. She'd been back to her own flat only the once to pack clothes for herself and to get her laptop.

Between them, they got everything inside and put away before Alana's teatime. The sky had clouded over and was now threatening rain, so Sophie fed her in the kitchen.

"Are you happy with a risotto for supper?" asked Samson, as he rooted around in the cupboards for inspiration.

"That would be lovely, but you don't have to cook for me! I can pop out to a supermarket and pick something up for myself."

"I'm going to be cooking anyway, and it's your first night here," replied Samson amiably.

It was rather sweet how domesticated he was and how hard he was trying to be agreeable and build a friendly relationship with her. He was going out of his way to make her feel welcome.

"What if I run out and get us a bottle of wine as my contribution? It'll give me a chance to have a little wander around the area."

"That is a very good idea. There's a Tesco five minutes' walk away, turn left out of the house and right at the end of the road. Keep going and you'll come to it. I'll finish off with Alana if you like."

"Thanks. Red or white?"

"White. And could you pick up some parmesan?"

"Sure." Sophie grabbed her purse, pleased at the ready domesticity and ease of their new-found truce. Long may it last . . .

The rain held off for her little jaunt. Already after only a short time looking after Alana, it felt like a wonderful luxury to be out by herself, to merely grab her purse and her mobile and walk out of the house alone and explore a little.

She'd been right about the area being far nicer than that around Natasha's flat, and she enjoyed checking out the beautiful, old houses. She passed a park with a playground, thinking she might take Alana there the next day, and felt the lightest she had since the night Natasha had died.

* * *

Sophie got back and ran Alana's bath and asked Samson if he'd like to wash the baby.

"If you teach me how!" he answered and she laughed. Who would have thought a month ago that anyone would ask her to instruct them in anything to do with caring for a tiny person?

She called Samson in to see his little girl splashing away happily in the water and showed him how to wash her hair and make her giggle by squirting her with her rubber duck. She could tell he was nervous lifting the slippery baby out of the tub, but he managed it and wrapped her in a towel to carry her through to her bedroom. He even seemed to take pleasure choosing what sleepy suit to put his little girl in. He was so gentle with Alana, seeming to marvel at her.

Samson read *The Gruffalo* to Alana while Sophie went downstairs to sort out the bedtime bottle. As she added the scoops of formula to the water, she couldn't help but notice how relaxed she felt. It was so different having someone else to share the bedtime routine with.

She'd worried she might feel jealous or usurped having Samson take part in everything with Alana, but, for the moment at least, she didn't. She felt less alone in her troubles.

* * *

Samson tidied up and got Alana's cot ready for her while Sophie gave the baby her bottle. Sophie insisted the room be darkened for the last bottle of the day, it was what the experts said, so

Samson was working by the weak beam of a night light. Sophie knew the fact he wasn't complaining about this, was a real testament to how much he wanted them staying with him to work.

Once the room was ready for Alana to sleep in, he came over and bent down to kiss his daughter on the head. Sophie moved as far back as possible to give him space, but found she held her breath until he stood up again and went downstairs to begin cooking.

She put Alana to bed and then went downstairs to join Samson. She was a little apprehensive as she approached the kitchen: would things be awkward without Alana there? Would they have anything left to talk about, or would they sit in silence as they ate their meal as quickly as possible?

She needn't have worried. Samson seemed very happy to chat about Sophie's favourite subject, Alana, and was clearly continuing his efforts to help her feel relaxed.

The risotto was delicious and Sophie thoroughly enjoyed being cooked for twice in one day. "Who taught you to be so handy in the kitchen?" she asked between mouthfuls.

"My mum. She was determined that when I left home I'd know how to make myself a decent meal. Personally, I think it was so she could get me cooking for everyone once a week and claim it was for my own good."

"Well, I for one am very grateful to her."

"Me too deep down — it does come in handy."

"I'm rubbish in the kitchen," admitted Sophie. "Thank goodness for jars of baby food."

Their conversation was interrupted by some snuffles down the baby monitor. It was much more sensitive than the cheap model her sister had and had a screen so they would see what Alana was up to, which was a little disconcerting if Sophie were honest. It was amusing to see how wriggly her niece was once they thought she was all settled though.

Samson appeared mesmerised by his daughter's antics, but finally managed to pull his attention away from it. "Sorry," he said, "I can't seem not to watch, maybe the screen is a little much."

"You really want to do your best for her, don't you?" said Sophie quietly. Seeing him in this light made her consider what a brilliant ally Samson could be, someone who could help and support her with the enormous, and sometimes frankly overwhelming, task of bringing up Alana.

"Yes, I do. I feel terrible I missed out on the first part of her life."

"It doesn't sound like it was entirely your fault," Sophie said, fairly.

"Natasha must have had some reason for not telling me when she found out she was pregnant. Some reason why she thought I shouldn't know, and she and Alana would be better off without me."

"Maybe it wasn't anything to do with you. Maybe she was confused and scared and as time went on, she didn't know how to tell you." Or me, Sophie mused. Not that she was prepared to tell Samson that.

"Perhaps," he said, not sounding convinced.

"Well . . . we'll never know the reason. But she was very independent and liked to do things her way."

"She certainly did," said Samson with a smile.

Sophie felt an unexpected surge of jealousy at the thought of Natasha and Samson together but did her best to shake it off. How could she be jealous of someone who was dead? And of her own sister?

They washed and tidied up together once they'd finished eating, but Sophie was very careful to keep her distance physically. It was way too confusing when they got too close to each other.

"I've got some stuff on a building project I'm working on which I ought to do if you're OK?"

"Of course, don't worry about me!" Sophie said immediately. She was secretly glad to have some time to herself to process exactly what had happened that day. Part of her was worried she'd acted too hastily and needed to be reassured by going over the options again in her head.

"You're very welcome to use my Netflix account if you want to commandeer the television," Samson offered.

Actually, Sophie thought, she'd love to relax in front of the TV, but she'd feel weird doing it in Samson's home. She wasn't comfortable enough there yet.

"No thanks, I think I'll finish sorting out my room and have a read and an early night. It's been a busy day."

"Sure. You know where I am if you need me," said Samson, "Do you want to take the baby monitor?"

"If you don't mind," she said. "Alana doesn't tend to wake in the night, thankfully."

"I guess I missed the months of night feeds," Samson commented.

"Yeah . . ." She had no idea what to say in this situation and was grateful when Samson spoke.

"Anyway, sleep well, I guess I'll see you in the morning."

Sophie went up to her room and fiddled around putting away the last of the things she'd brought with her. Then she got out her laptop, planning to do some research into some freelance work, but it was only when she had the computer all set up and had got comfortable on the bed with it that she realised she didn't have the Wi-Fi password. She umm-ed and ah-ed, but couldn't bring herself to interrupt Samson. She closed down her laptop and read until she heard him moving around, going to the bathroom and then into his bedroom. She put on her pyjamas and snuck out to use the bathroom herself, pausing by Alana's door, but deciding, as much as she'd like to see her niece, it wasn't worth risking waking her up.

She hurried back to her bedroom, and settled into bed, grateful Samson wasn't in the room next door but was much further up the hall. It would be very strange to be able to hear him moving around as he prepared for the night.

She lay down and tried to get to sleep, but it was too quiet without Alana's snufflings beside her. She'd only just got used to Alana's night-time noises and to sleeping in the same room as a baby, and now it was suddenly all change again. She hoped this change was very much for the good.

CHAPTER 6

Now that she was no longer living in it, Sophie was anxious to get on with clearing out Natasha's flat. She didn't have a great deal of time before she needed to hand the keys back to the council, and she felt the job was hanging over her. Also, she didn't have any work lined up at the moment, but hopefully would soon, so this seemed like the ideal opportunity to get on with the task.

She was out of bed early the following morning and in the shower before Alana woke up: there was no way she was facing Samson at the breakfast table in her pyjamas and with unbrushed teeth.

Samson looked gorgeously ruffled when he emerged as she was preparing a bottle for a rather grumpy Alana.

"Would you like me to take her?" asked Samson, stretching and showing a hint of toned, tanned stomach when his T-shirt rode up. Sophie handed Alana over gratefully but without words. She was feeling rather warm for some reason.

"Can I give her the bottle?" Samson asked.

"Certainly." Sophie handed him the ready formula. "Would you like a cup of tea?"

"Absolutely."

Sophie pottered around Samson's kitchen making them both drinks and then toast with butter and marmite. It all felt very 'happy families', but surreal. Only the morning before she'd been living in a tiny council flat coping with a newly acquired baby completely by herself.

"What are you up to today?" Samson asked.

"I'm going to tackle Natasha's flat. The sooner it's done, the sooner I can hand the keys back and sort out my own place I guess."

"Would you like some help?" Samson asked immediately. "It sounds like a big job to do by yourself. And an upsetting one . . ."

"I'll be OK," she said automatically, although, all of a sudden, what she wanted was for Samson to be with her and not to be alone going through her sister's things. "Maybe you could watch Alana for a while?"

"Alana and I can come with you. She'll be fine if we take a few bits for her to play with, and her old cot will be there for her nap. And anything you want to keep, you can store down in the cellar here — there's plenty of room. Please let me help. I'm not comfortable with you doing this by yourself."

"Thank you," said Sophie honestly, feeling a huge weight lift. It would still be a horrible thing to do, but she already knew it would be made easier by having Samson there. She'd be less likely to wallow too if she had someone else with her and it would get it all over with quicker.

Once they'd finished breakfast, they loaded up Samson's battered pick-up truck with cleaning supplies and Sophie grabbed anything she suspected they'd need for Alana. Samson found a few boxes in his loft which he thought would be handy for packing things up in.

They set to work as soon as they reached the flat, beginning in the kitchen. The paperwork in the drawer Sophie shoved in a box; she'd need to go through that all properly and check everyone who needed to be notified about Natasha's death had been. As it seemed Natasha hadn't cooked much, their work in that room was finished quickly, it was the cleaning of it that took the most time.

The same was true of the minuscule bathroom, and once they'd finished that, they filled up the truck with anything which was to be kept and drove back to Samson's house. Sophie was tired but glad the majority of the cleaning had been done. One more day would finish the job, and Samson said he and Alana were more than happy to help out again. They'd both been good company, and their presence served to keep Sophie's spirits up and prevent her becoming too maudlin. Samson had put the radio on as a distraction which helped, and working quickly to keep up with him helped to move things along swiftly.

The next morning, Samson dropped Mutt off with one of his friends so he wouldn't be left by himself for hours again.

"Hop on in!" Samson called out cheerfully when he returned to pick them up. Learning her lesson from a bored Alana the day before, which had led to the prolonged singing of 'Twinkle, Twinkle Little Star' and a lot of pans being banged with wooden spoons, Sophie made sure she brought along plenty of snacks and the dreaded noisy baby walker.

Sophie packed and cleaned while Samson made trips back and forth to the truck and put any rubbish into bags ready to take to the dump. Again, they made a surprisingly good team, though Sophie wasn't in the mood to talk. It hurt her that nothing in her sister's flat held any significance to her. None of the mementoes from her sister's travels which Natasha had scattered about her home meant anything to Sophie. She didn't have a favourite mug Natasha would always make her coffee in when she visited, or a best spot on the sofa in the sitting room when they watched a movie together. The only things she was anxious to keep were anything she felt Natasha had chosen especially for Alana.

They moved into the bedroom and looked around. "I'll take the cot to the dump along with the bed if you like?" Samson suggested.

"The bed can go, but I'll keep hold of the cot."

"But she's got a cot at my house."

"Yes, but we don't know how long we're going to be staying with you," Sophie replied automatically. "It's silly to get rid of a perfectly good cot."

"It seems a bit rickety to me," responded Samson, giving it a tug. In fairness, it did wobble more than it should have, but Sophie wasn't in the mood to be reasonable about this: he was putting down something Natasha had chosen for her daughter. It was probably the cot Alana had slept in all her life.

"I'm keeping it," Sophie said firmly.

"Where are you going to put it? It's pretty big."

"You said I could keep whatever I wanted at your house!"

Samson seemed as if he were going to argue with her, but thought better of it. "Maybe I could dismantle it and put it in the cellar until you decide what to do with it," he said reasonably.

Sophie managed to stop herself from continuing to argue. Even in her upset state, she knew Samson was being more than fair, and it was lovely of him to help her like he was. This was her not him. The cot wasn't nearly as nice as the one he'd bought. It must have been second-hand when Natasha got it. There was no real reason to keep it. She would want to replace it herself even if they didn't stay at Samson's for long.

"It can go to the dump," she said quietly.

"Are you sure?" Samson asked.

Sophie nodded as her emotions got the better of her and she began to cry.

Samson came straight over and held her, saying nothing, but rubbing her back soothingly until she was done.

"Better?" he asked gently as she dried her eyes on her sleeve.

"A bit." She forced a small smile. "There was so much I didn't know about Natasha. We weren't all that close, and now I'll never know her. Her stuff here . . . it seems like the last chance I have to discover more and to be able to tell Alana about her mother and give her an insight into what Natasha was like. And to show Alana her mother loved her."

"I wish I could help you more, but I didn't know Natasha well. I never even came in here," Samson said. He stood quietly, thinking for a moment. "When my grandma passed away, my mum kept her perfume to remember her by. That might be nice for Alana. And possibly some of her clothes? I can't see any photos out, but maybe she's got some hidden away somewhere?"

Sophie nodded gratefully, her chest tight at the thought of Alana growing up with no memory of her mother, but gave her eyes a last wipe, determined to be pragmatic. Getting upset in front of Samson was embarrassing and she didn't want Alana to see her crying. "The good thing about her not having much stuff is we should be able to clear the last of it in a couple of loads."

"It doesn't look like she was sentimental," said Samson.

"It seems not . . ."

"Actually, there's a women's shelter near here which would be grateful for any of the furniture you didn't want to keep."

"All of it can go. Could you give them a call and see if we can drop it off today?" asked Sophie decisively, trying to get organised, at least about the things which could hold little, if any, emotional value.

"Sure," said Samson, taking out his mobile and doing a web search for the number.

It wasn't until they'd got the final load of the day on the pick-up truck, and Samson had driven off with it, taking Alana with him, that Sophie pulled out an old shoebox from the back of the built-in wardrobe in Natasha's room. Lifting the lid hopefully, she found what she'd been searching for: the photos and little keepsakes she knew Alana would so value when she was older and desperate to discover more about the mother she lost when she was too young to remember her.

Sophie sat cross-legged on the floor, her back resting against the wall, and delved in.

The box was stuffed full of a complete hodgepodge of ticket stubs, photos and scraps of paper. Sophie smiled as she picked up a picture of Natasha with her arms around two friends Sophie didn't know, grinning at the camera. She put it aside in a 'keep' pile. Perhaps it wasn't the most productive 'sorting' she could be tackling right now, but it was what she needed to do.

She uncovered some treasures, chief of them Alana's hospital wristband from when she was born. Other mementoes — tickets to bands Sophie had never heard of, photos of people she didn't know — served to reinforce the hurt that it had been a very long time since Sophie played any sort of part in her sister's life.

Samson came in as she was tidying everything up; she'd kept practically all of the box. The contents had been carefully gathered and each thing must have meant a lot to Natasha. It would be the best window into her mother's life that she could give Alana.

"Are you all right?" Samson asked gently, touching her on the shoulder.

"I think so," she said, getting up.

"Are you finished?"

"Well . . . no. I got sidetracked." She raised the box in her hands in explanation. "But I want to get back to make tea for Alana. Thanks for the last couple of days. You were right, it would have been far worse doing it on my own. I was glad you were here."

"It's fine, I was happy to help, and it's good you've found the keepsakes you wanted for Alana," he said sadly. "I've taken the last of the stuff to the refuge, so let's load up the truck with what you want to keep."

They locked up the flat and posted the keys through the letterbox. Sophie probably would have found it hard to pull herself away, but Alana was tired and hungry and began to cry, pulling Sophie back to the present and away from her sad thoughts of the past.

It was a pitifully small amount in the back of the truck Sophie thought to herself as she held the box of memories safely on her lap, but she had what was important and she was glad she'd kept it.

* * *

A couple of hours later, Alana was safely asleep in her cot. Sophie and Samson had eaten some over-cooked pasta and pesto Sophie had made as a thank you to Samson for all his help that day, and then felt the need to apologise for. Samson had gone to work in his office upstairs. Sophie suspected he had quite a bit to catch up on from the last couple of days, not that he'd mentioned it.

He'd promised to look after Alana the next day and lend Sophie his truck so she could drive to London, pack up her own stuff and meet some estate agents. She wanted to get her flat rented out as soon as possible so she'd have some income coming in. She'd need to clean the whole place thoroughly, and she had guys coming to perform gas and electric safety checks and a handyman to sort out a couple of jobs which needed doing. It was going to be a long day.

She was surprised at herself for not being more concerned about leaving Alana with Samson for so long, especially with Mutt around, though even Sophie had to admit the dog and her niece made a cute pair. But Samson had promised to call if there was a problem and had even allowed her to write out Alana's schedule for him to abide by. He'd then stuck it in prime position on the fridge.

She'd have to make sure Samson got some proper time to himself the day after or he'd be regretting ever asking the pair of them to move in!

Sophie decided to take the opportunity of having the kitchen table to herself to check again through the box she'd brought back from Natasha's flat.

She emptied it all onto the table and began sorting it into piles. Finally, as she was nearing the very end of her search, she found what she'd been searching for: a single selfie of Natasha and Alana together. Natasha was kissing her daughter on the cheek, and Alana was giggling like crazy.

She was smiling at it when Samson came in. "I fancied a cup of tea, would you like one?" he asked, then seeing her face, "What have you got?"

Sophie held the photo out to him to see. "That's lovely," he said.

"Isn't it? I'm so pleased I found it."

Samson switched on the kettle, and indicated to it, reminding Sophie of his earlier question. "Oh, no thanks, not for me," said Sophie, noticing the time. She wanted to be off early the next morning so should be getting to bed.

She tidied up the table, deciding to keep everything in the container she'd found it in, as that was where Natasha had chosen to store her treasures. Pausing before returning the photo of Natasha and Alana to the box, she decided to leave it on the side. She'd have a think about what best to do with it.

CHAPTER 7

When Sophie got back the following evening it was after ten. She was tired but very pleased with what she'd managed to get done. She'd handed keys to her flat over to the estate agents so they could take care of their side of things. It would be available for potential tenants to view in a week or so apparently. Everything was packed and sorted, it would only need one more, very laden, journey back to Samson's house she thought and she'd be done. She'd been ruthless with her culling and the furniture was staying in place, so everything was practically ready to go. The income from the let would comfortably cover her mortgage payments with quite a bit left over. She'd even remembered to call the number Yvonne the social worker had given her and left a message giving Samson's house as Alana and her new address.

It would be good to have more of her things around her again, even if she wasn't living in her own home. She had a load of stuff in the cab of the pick-up truck outside, but it would have to wait until the morning to be brought in; she didn't want to wake Alana by banging around dragging stuff up the stairs. She was sure the boxes under the tarp on the truck bed would be fine where they were: the weather was dry and it was a nice neighbourhood.

The downstairs was in darkness when she opened the front door, presumably Samson had gone to bed already. She dumped her bag on the floor of the hallway, exhausted after her long day and from dealing with the aftermath of her emotions from the day before, but sighed, turned back around and picked it up again: this was Samson's hallway, she couldn't leave her stuff lying around everywhere. She crept up the stairs as quietly as she could so as not to wake Samson or Alana. As she snuck past her niece's room though, she couldn't resist opening the door to take a peek at the sleeping little girl. She'd missed her and was sad to have lost out on her bedtime routine.

Sophie couldn't help herself and slipped in, tiptoeing over to the cot. Alana was fast asleep, clutching her toy rabbit. Sophie tentatively pulled the blanket up a little and placed a gentle kiss on her forehead. As she turned to leave, she noticed an unfamiliar shape on the top of the chest of drawers and went closer to investigate. By the light from the hallway, she could see it was a pretty silver frame holding the selfie photo of Natasha and Alana she'd left out. She smiled at Samson's thoughtful gesture.

Walking back out into the hallway, she bumped into the man himself. Sophie gave a little jump of surprise. "I thought you were asleep."

"I was in my bedroom and heard a noise from Alana's room so I came to investigate."

"I saw what you did with the photo . . ."

"Was it all right?" Samson asked quickly, clearly afraid he'd offended Sophie.

"It's lovely," reassured Sophie. "Really kind."

"I put it so Alana could see it from her cot."

"That was sweet of you."

Samson looked embarrassed. "How did it go today? Did you get everything done you wanted to?"

"It was good, and, amazingly, it all got done. Well, pretty much — it's piled in a corner ready, but I'll need to slip back for another load with the Toyota if that's OK?

I'm renting the flat out furnished so I didn't have to remove the furniture. Everything else is sorted! Hopefully, I'll have tenants soon."

"That's brilliant!"

"There's a load of boxes in the van. I'll bring them in tomorrow."

"Are you sure? I can give you a hand with it now?"

"Nah, it'll be safe enough out there until morning."

"OK, as long as you're sure . . ."

They stood awkwardly. Sophie longed to ask Samson if he'd like to join her for a cup of tea; she'd love to sit, chat, and then fill him in on the finer details of her day. She was nervous, but curiously excited about the life-changing moves she was making, though felt terribly guilty that it was all due to her sister's accident. It would be helpful to have someone to talk things through with, and she was learning to respect Samson and valued his advice hugely. She was trying to get up the courage to ask him, to work out the right words with the right level of nonchalance when Samson said, "Well, good night then. I left you some spaghetti Bolognese if you want it, it's in the fridge."

"Thank you," Sophie said, hiding her disappointment, but Samson was already heading back to his bedroom.

She went back downstairs by herself and heated up the leftover food, which she ate watching some Netflix in her bedroom. She heard Samson moving around after she'd gone to bed, but she didn't get up again. She was in her pyjamas and maybe Samson had waited until she was out of the way to go downstairs so he could have the place to himself for a bit. More deflated than she ought to be, she lay in bed trying to buoy herself up with her achievements today until sleep came.

* * *

Sophie didn't wake up until almost half eight, by far the longest lie-in she'd had since she'd met her niece. She lay in bed for a moment, luxuriating in not being woken up by a crying baby far earlier than this, before fully registering the time and beginning to worry something was wrong. Why hadn't Alana woken up yet? She rushed out along the hall and into Alana's room to the baby's cot. Alana wasn't in it. Sophie breathed a sigh of relief. Samson had obviously beaten her to it this morning and had been kind enough to let her stay in bed.

The now-framed photograph again caught her eye as she turned to leave the room and she reflected once more on how good Samson was being to both her and Alana. Maybe they could all do something together today if Samson wasn't too busy. They could take Alana swimming, or to the aquarium Sophie had read about.

She returned to her room and grabbed her super comfy but extremely faded and huge, dressing gown. She'd decided to brave Samson seeing her in her nightclothes. They were sharing a house after all and it was going to happen sooner or later.

With a smile on her face anticipating seeing her niece, and, yes, Samson, Sophie hurried down the stairs, pulling her hair back into a ponytail as she went. However, her mood abruptly changed when she saw a woman she didn't know sitting at the kitchen table next to Alana.

Samson was by the kettle making tea. He turned when Alana gave an excited squeak at the sight of her aunt. The woman at the table peered up at Sophie, her face impassive. She was tall from what Sophie could make out and very beautiful, with long, flowing red hair and pale, pale skin. She immediately reminded Sophie of some sort of Celtic nymph as she perched on a chair, picking at a bowl of chopped fruit.

"Morning, Sophie," said Samson cheerfully. "Did you sleep well?"

"Yes, thanks," said Sophie automatically, trying to work out the scene in front of her.

"This is Helena," Samson said in introduction. "Helena, this is Sophie, Alana's aunt."

"Nice to meet you, Helena," said Sophie politely, and held out her hand for Helena to shake.

Helena took it limply. "So, I understand you're living with my boyfriend," she said bluntly, while she artfully teased her tumbling locks into a cool topknot.

Sophie turned desperately to Samson for help, but he just looked uncomfortable and went back to fiddling around making tea. Unfortunately for him, Sophie wasn't about to let him get away with not explaining properly what was going on though.

"I wasn't aware Samson had a girlfriend," she pointedly responded.

She turned to make a fuss of Alana and could feel the glare Helena was giving Samson fill the room.

"I've been away," Helena snapped. "Filming in Prague."

"Helena's a model," Samson explained.

Of course, she would be, thought Sophie.

"Has Alana had her bottle?" she asked, trying to act as normally as possible, despite the tumult of emotions running through her.

"Yeah, a while ago," Samson replied. "I was going to give her some porridge in a minute."

"I can do that if you like?" offered Sophie.

Before Samson could respond, Helena said, "Great, so we can finally get going then." She got up, and marched out of the room.

"We were hoping to fit in some surfing this morning if you're OK to have Alana?" explained Samson.

"Of course, no problem." Sophie trusted she was managing to completely hide the disappointment she felt.

Samson turned to leave, but stopped. "About Helena . . ." he began but was interrupted by the woman herself calling for him. "Sorry, I'd better go," he said and left the kitchen.

Sophie put on a podcast for some company and set about giving her niece her breakfast. Once Alana had her porridge and was happily mushing banana into her tray, Sophie got herself some cereal and sat down heavily at the table. What on earth had happened? Here she was fantasising about Samson when she hadn't even considered the possibility he might not be single despite him being kind, handsome, fit, intelligent and wealthy. But why hadn't he told her he had a girlfriend? Surely that was a piece of information which should have come up in conversation in the last few days? They were living in the same house for goodness' sake! Presumably, Helena had been in Samson's bedroom last night when Sophie got in and Samson had chatted to her in the hallway outside Alana's room. Thank goodness she hadn't asked him to come downstairs and join her for a cup of tea! What would his response have been? "Sorry, I'm going to go back to bed with my model girlfriend and her awesome hair, but enjoy your hot beverage."

She heard Samson and Helena coming downstairs again. Samson came in and kissed Alana goodbye. "I'll see you guys later," he said.

"Sure," Sophie replied, not looking him in the eye, but doing her best to sound bright and breezy.

"Hey, maybe you could both come down to the beach? Alana, wouldn't you like to see Daddy surf?"

The baby giggled and waved her arms in excitement.

"I don't know . . ." Sophie, tried to swiftly think of a plausible excuse as to why she and Alana couldn't possibly go to the beach.

They were interrupted by a furious Helena at the kitchen door. "The truck's full of boxes and bags," she huffed.

"Sorry!" Sophie got up immediately. "That's my stuff. It was late when I got back so I didn't unload it — I'll do it now."

"You let her borrow your truck?" asked Helena incredulously, her eyes flashing dangerously.

"She was clearing out her flat. I thought she might need the extra space."

"You never let me borrow your truck!"

"You've never asked me if you can borrow my truck."

"Because I know you wouldn't let me!"

Sophie wished the ground would open up and swallow her whole, or that at least everyone would stop talking about her like she wasn't there.

Finally, Samson recalled Sophie's presence. "It won't take me two minutes to empty it," he said, ending the argument.

"I can do it," said Sophie, lamely.

"It's all right," Samson said, giving her a reassuring smile. "You watch Alana."

He left to unpack the truck. Helena stayed and glared at Sophie from the doorway. Sophie ignored her and chatted to Alana as she cleaned the little girl up.

It didn't take Samson long to clear the truck and to call out, "All done, let's get going!"

Helena spun around and stomped off, not saying anything to Sophie.

"Well, she was a delight, wasn't she?" muttered Sophie to Alana, not quite under her breath enough she worried, when she heard Samson say, "We're off then. Call if you need anything." He was standing in the doorway, and she was sure she could see a little frown on his face which he quickly tried to hide.

"Great, have fun!" mumbled Sophie, again not daring to meet his eyes in case she started blushing even more than she already was.

* * *

Sophie had a quick shower with Alana watching her from her bouncer and then set about trying to decide what she and her niece would do for the day. She figured they both deserved a bit of fun but was there truly much you could do with an eight-month-old? Would it be worth taking her to the aquarium? She knew part of her reluctance was caused by the fact that she wouldn't have Samson with her and she'd been excited about spending the day with him, not solely because it would be easier to look after Alana with another adult around, but because she was enjoying his company.

Having said that, from a practical point of view, there was no way she was going to attempt to take Alana swimming without help. And she was also absolutely determined to stay well away from the beach.

Maybe it didn't need to be a full day out, which, to be honest, she'd never done with Alana before and would mean messing terribly with her routine, but something different and exciting enough to show Samson she could manage everything, and that she and Alana could do perfectly well without him.

Sophie decided she'd start small and take Alana to the park she'd spotted a couple of days before. They'd come back for Alana's nap and lunch, and then maybe head out somewhere else. She could use the time while her niece slept to send some emails to businesses she thought might be interested in her accounting services.

She got Alana ready and checked the changing bag was fully stocked and contained everything she could possibly need. It didn't, so she had to repack. She suspected Samson had 'borrowed' things the day before and hadn't replaced them.

Finally, they were ready to go. It was overcast but wasn't supposed to rain. Sophie packed Alana's raincoat and the buggy's rain cover just in case, as well as a sunhat and sunblock.

The park was surprisingly busy when they reached it, full of mums with their babies. Presumably, a lot of them dropped older children off at school and then took the little ones to have a run around in the playground. Sophie almost turned right around and went home. All the mothers seemed older than her and to know each other and were chatting in little groups. They also universally gave the appearance of knowing what they were doing with their children. But Alana spotted the swings and started bouncing up and down in her pram with excitement. Sophie didn't have the heart to upset her niece by heading home without at least letting her have a little go.

Sophie parked the buggy by the entrance to the playground and lifted Alana out. There was a baby swing free and she popped Alana in, before becoming suddenly petrified she would topple out. She debated taking her out again but anticipated a major meltdown if she did. She gave the swing a tentative push and Alana's face broke out into a grin, making Sophie's heart lift: it was moments like this which made her think maybe she wasn't doing such a bad job after all.

The swing next to Alana's became available and a tall young woman with short, curly brown hair brought her grizzling, chubby little boy over to use it. He had the same hair as his mum and was a little older than Alana from what Sophie could tell.

As soon as his mother started to push the swing the boy began to cheer up and Sophie heard his mother mutter, "Thank goodness for that."

Sophie turned to look at her, and the woman smiled back.

"It's been one of those mornings," she explained.

Sophie nodded as knowledgeably as she could, trying to give the impression she'd been parenting for more than three weeks.

"How old's your daughter?" asked the woman.

"Eight months," replied Sophie, deciding not to go into the whole story of her actual relationship with Alana with a complete stranger. Was she really having her first 'baby' conversation with a mum?

"Olly's nearly ten months. He's so busy now he's crawling everywhere, it's exhausting! I can't believe how fast he can move."

"Alana's not crawling yet, but she has started trying to pull herself up onto her hands and knees."

"Make the most of it before she starts! I'm Julia. I haven't seen you around. Have you recently moved to the area?"

"Yeah, from London. I'm Sophie."

"Well it's pretty good here for baby stuff. Some of the groups can be a bit cliquey though. There's a fab one in the church hall on West Street this afternoon. Have you heard of it? Olly loves it because he gets to do all sorts of messy stuff, and I love it because I don't have to clean the paint off my own kitchen walls!"

"I haven't had a chance to check out any baby groups yet," confessed Sophie.

"Come along later if you're free?"

"I will, thanks," said Sophie, thrilled she may very well have made her first 'Mummy Friend'.

* * *

By the time Sophie put Alana in her highchair for her tea, she thought she could definitely say she'd made a pal in Julia. She'd been brave and gone to the baby group, but she needn't have worried about not fitting in; everyone had been so nice and friendly. It was really good to chat with other women and it made her miss her friends from London. Her life now felt so removed from theirs but she resolved to do better about keeping in touch with them.

She'd also loved seeing Alana with the other babies; she'd been so interested! Especially in Olly, who seemed determined to bring her as many toy cars as possible, show-ing off his impressive crawling skills. Developing his courting technique early? she mused.

Alana had had a little nap in her buggy afterwards when she and Julia walked back to Julia's for a coffee.

Julia's home was a large flat she shared with her husband in a converted Edwardian house. "We're hoping to move next year," she explained. "It would be lovely to live some-where with a garden."

The babies were popped on a brightly coloured playmat with plenty of toys in the centre of the large sitting room to keep them amused, while the grown-ups drank their drinks and made short work of a plate of custard creams.

"So," said Julia, taking a sip from her coffee, "what made you move to Brighton?"

Sophie considered fobbing Julia off, but she may as well get used to telling people about her situation, and it would be good to get someone else's views on it, and so, taking a deep breath first, Sophie explained about Natasha, Alana and Samson. "That does sound complicated."

"It's not the easiest of situations," Sophie admitted, "but we seem to be muddling through. I'm still very much finding my feet with the whole baby business."

Julia stood up and came over to Sophie to hug her. "You're doing an amazing job," she said. "Alana is so lucky to have you."

Sophie bit her lip. She hadn't quite realised how much she needed to hear she was doing OK. Most days she still felt she had no idea what she was doing with her niece.

She left her new friend's home a little while later feeling a lot lighter, and glad she'd filled up her day without Samson, and even spent some of it not thinking about him and his model girlfriend.

CHAPTER 8

Alana was finishing her tea when Samson arrived home. He came straight into the kitchen to find them and gave his daughter an affectionate kiss on the head.

"Hiya," he said. "Have you two had a good day?"

"Yes, thanks," replied Sophie. "Is Helena not with you?"

"Nah, she's gone back to her own place. She wanted to unpack properly I think . . ."

"Right . . ."

"Um . . ." He looked at her awkwardly. "I'm sorry she wasn't very friendly this morning."

"It's fine, don't worry about it," said Sophie shortly.

"She's finding it difficult to adjust to Alana I guess," Samson explained. "It was a surprise for both of us — finding out I was a father, I mean. And it's not what she signed up for, you know? She's not a baby person."

Sophie had no desire to hear any more about Helena or how hard she was finding things. She gave a non-committal, "Hmm . . ."

Realising Sophie wasn't in a very good mood with him, Samson continued, "I should have told you about her before."

Worried Samson would assume she was jealous unless she corrected him quickly, Sophie responded, "Your private life is your own, it's nothing to do with me." She was very careful to fuss around cleaning up Alana, and to avoid eye contact with Samson. "Actually, as you're here, it might be a good time to work out how we're going to organise things around the house."

Samson appeared a bit taken aback by this turn of events. "How do you mean?"

"Well," said Sophie, thinking on her feet, "Maybe we could have a weekly schedule, so we know who's looking after Alana and when, and the times either one of us will be unavailable. We should have a meeting each Sunday to plan it."

"Right. That's certainly very . . . organised."

"And would it be possible for you to clear a shelf in the fridge for my food?"

"Sure . . ."

"Great. I'd also like to pay my way. I don't expect a free ride."

"That's not necessary."

"It is," said Sophie firmly.

"OK," Samson said resignedly. "How much were you thinking?"

Sophie was thrown: she hadn't thought any of this through, and certainly didn't have any figure in mind. She knew it would be a good idea to put some distance between them.

"£200?" she suggested.

"A month?"

"A week," she replied determinedly, swiftly doing some calculations in her head. She had savings, and hopefully her flat in London would be rented out soon and she'd have some work. She should be able to afford it. "I insist."

"All right," said Samson, with a shrug. "But there's no need."

"I'd feel more comfortable."

"Take whatever shelf in the fridge you want and I'll clear you out some cupboard space later," Samson offered. "Shall I take Alana for her bath?"

"Yeah, thanks, that would be great. I'll pop out to the supermarket. Do you need anything?"

"Nope, I'm good. I was going to make a curry tonight if you'd like some."

Sophie's stomach rumbled at the thought. She wished Samson weren't such a good cook, it would make his food much easier to resist if he wasn't. But he had a girlfriend, a very beautiful girlfriend, and Sophie could feel that the more time she spent around Samson, the more she was attracted to him, especially when she saw how sweet he was with Alana. She needed to take a step back, mark out some boundaries, for her own good. Her mind was also very much focusing on the problem of Alana's future still not being properly decided: they couldn't stay living with Samson for ever, but if he turned around and tried to push for sole custody of Alana, as would probably be his right, it would be so much harder to fight him were she to allow her feelings to get even more out of control. Her priority was keeping Alana with her, or at least having shared custody, and she needed to remember that.

"No, I'll sort myself. Thanks, though," she replied.

* * *

Sophie felt more than a little silly cooking her frozen pizza while Samson made a delicious smelling sag aloo complete with fragrant basmati rice, yoghurt and poppadoms. But she was determined to stick to her guns: they needed space, it would be far too easy to settle into some domestic routine, too close to pretending to be a couple. Her feelings would end up being crushed and it wasn't right with Samson having a girlfriend — she went by an unwritten code that she'd never go after another woman's man. Sure, Helena hadn't exactly been welcoming towards her, but it must be a difficult situation; it's only natural it would take her a while to get used to things. As Samson had said, Helena certainly hadn't expected him to have a baby, and then to have the baby and her aunt move in with him. Maybe, given time, she'd become friendlier, but Sophie supposed she couldn't blame Helena for being off with her — she'd most likely act the same way if their roles were reversed.

And the niggling thought of earlier, of Samson pushing for full custody of Alana, wouldn't stop spiralling around and around her head. In their new-found rapport and the sheer busyness of the last weeks, she'd managed to largely push it to the back of her mind, but today's wobble in their relationship had once again sprouted that seed of worry — he seemed nice and genuine, and she was certain he adored Alana, but what would happen if he decided he'd had enough of having his daughter's aunt hanging around? Or if he and Helena got married? What rights did she have? She wasn't even sure and she didn't like that. She was used to having everything ordered and knowing where she stood. This situation made Sophie feel totally out of her comfort zone.

Samson tried to make conversation, asking about her day and wanting to know all about Alana at the baby group, but Sophie felt too uncomfortable and wary to relax into small talk and was relieved when she'd eaten her food and could make her excuses and escape to the sanctuary of her bedroom.

Her sleep was far more interrupted than the night before. She wished Samson had told her about Helena when they'd first met. Then she would have properly known the situation she was getting herself into when she agreed to move into his house.

Working herself up further, she irrationally felt she should leave, but she couldn't afford to live anywhere else at the moment, and she was loath to uproot Alana again — the baby adored her father, despite the short amount of time she'd known him, and seemed to have settled brilliantly into his home. And what would she do about childcare without Samson so handily around?

She also didn't know how Samson would react if she said she and Alana were leaving. He was completely serious about wanting a relationship with his daughter, and Sophie didn't want him to decide she was trying to stop this and potentially end up in an unnecessary legal battle, which she could well lose if it were discovered how short a time she'd known her niece.

Her one other, inconceivable, option would be to move out by herself and leave Alana with Samson. That would certainly make it a lot easier for her to work, but there was no way Sophie could ever consider it. She loved Alana. Sophie was now the closest thing her niece had to a mother, and she was determined to play a major part in her upbringing.

No, the best plan was to stay with Samson for the time being, at least until she was more financially stable. Then she could continue with the process of getting a formal arrangement worked out, so she had some official guardianship powers.

She eventually managed to get to sleep in the early hours of the morning, when her frazzled mind finally gave in to her body's need for rest.

* * *

Sophie forced herself up early the next morning, resolute that today she was not going to be blindsided in her pyjamas again by random beautiful girlfriends in the kitchen.

She heard Alana beginning to stir as she got out of a super quick shower. She hurried out of the bathroom wrapped in a towel, but Samson was already at her niece's bedroom door.

"I'll get her while you sort yourself out," he said gesturing to the towel turban on her head. Embarrassed at being caught looking a mess yet again, Sophie mumbled, "Thanks, I'll be down soon," as she scuttled to the safety of her room.

She actually took her time getting dressed and drying her hair, then put on some subtle make-up. Samson and Alana would be fine together for a few extra minutes, and she wanted to appear half-decent when she went downstairs.

Samson didn't hear her coming along the hall over the sound of the radio he had on and she stood in the kitchen doorway watching Samson and Alana together. Samson was giving his daughter her bottle. 'All You Need is Love' by the Beatles was playing, and Samson sang along softly to Alana. They both appeared mesmerised by one another; the bond between father and daughter was already so strong.

Sophie's heart ached. They seemed so perfect together, a little unit. She felt like a complete outsider and, for a brief moment, more alone than she'd ever felt before, even when she was living by herself after her parents had died. Samson and Alana didn't require her, especially with Helena able to take on the role of mother to her niece. Was she being a complete fool imagining Alana needed her at all?

* * *

Over the following week, Sophie did her best to keep her life as separate from Samson's as possible, while co-parenting Alana, even finally making the trip to London to finish emptying her flat using her own car, which had definitely been a squeeze. The large weekly schedule they'd hashed out, and she'd insistently stuck on the fridge, definitely helped.

Pleasingly, the feelers she'd put out yielded some accounting work. She officially registered herself as self-employed with the taxman and updated her LinkedIn profile. It felt like she was properly moving herself and Alana forward.

Helena was, unfortunately, around the house a lot, which made things extremely difficult. Sophie couldn't help but feel Samson's girlfriend was marking her territory. She was either lounging around in the kitchen, being cooked for by Samson and idly flicking through fashion magazines or contorting herself into bizarre yoga positions in the den and glaring at Sophie if she dared to bring Alana in to watch an episode of *Peppa Pig*. A cat would spend less time preening and lazing about.

Sophie was very grateful for her new friendship with Julia. She now braved taking Alana to a couple of baby groups each week, and either to the park or Julia's flat most days. She hadn't brought her friend round to Samson's house, worried Helena would be there. She'd explained how awkward her situation was to Julia, who'd proved a very good sounding board, preventing Sophie's tendency of introspection and over-analysing from completely driving her demented.

Returning from Julia's one afternoon, Sophie found Helena once again at the kitchen table. Samson was making tea and took Alana from Sophie when her mobile began ringing. Sophie went out into the garden to answer it.

When she returned to the kitchen a few minutes later, Samson was playing with Alana and Helena was fiddling with her phone.

"Are you able to look after Alana tomorrow?" Sophie asked hopefully. "That call was an old client of mine. He's leaving the company I used to work for and wants me to go to London to see what I can do for him. I'd be gone the whole day, but it should mean a nice lot of work coming my way."

"Oh! I'm sorry, but I can't," Samson answered. "I've got an inspection on an office building I've been consulting on. It's been organised for weeks and isn't something I can change. It's on the planner."

"Maybe my friend Julia could help . . ." Sophie was already dialling Julia's number and heading back out into the garden so she could make the call in private.

She returned, despondent, a couple of minutes later. She'd forgotten Julia was heading up to Yorkshire to visit her family.

"Any luck?" Samson asked.

"No. I'll call and see if there's any way it can be rescheduled." Sophie absentmindedly passed Alana a rice cake from an open packet on the table as she tried to figure out the best way to work things. She didn't want to lose what could be a very good client.

"Don't worry," said Samson, "we'll sort it. Um . . . have you got anything on tomorrow, Helena? I don't suppose you'd be able to do it?"

Sophie cringed inside: please let her be busy, please let her have to go to 'Super Power Pilates for Ridiculously Bendy People' or something.

"Sure, I'll babysit her," Helena said idly.

"Really? That'll be perfect!" and "Oh! Are you sure?" followed practically simultaneously from Samson and Sophie.

"I can babysit her tomorrow," Helena said slowly and clearly.

"Great — if that's OK?" Samson asked.

"I can reschedule I'm sure," Sophie said uncertainly. She didn't want to miss out on this opportunity, but at the same time how would Helena manage with Alana all day? She hadn't shown any interest in her boyfriend's child, hadn't even changed a nappy that Sophie knew of.

"For goodness' sake!" said Helena, impatiently. "It's a baby! It can't be that hard to keep an eye on her for a few hours. I'll call if there's a problem."

"Thanks." Samson went over and kissed Helena. "That's sweet of you. I'll get back as early as I can to take over."

"Yeah, thanks." Sophie, forced a smile. She felt sick at the thought of Helena looking after Alana. What did she know about caring for a baby, what if Alana got hurt? Or what if they ended up having an amazing time, and Alana preferred Helena to her? Helena and Samson would get married, and Alana would live with them and Sophie would be a random aunt Alana saw now and again.

Sophie knew she was overreacting to the situation but couldn't calm her mind.

"Do you want to feed Alana her tea?" Samson asked Helena, holding out a bowl of baby food.

"Ew, no," she said, waving her hands in the air. "I'm doing my nails."

Sophie managed to hide her pleasure — at least one of her concerns could be ticked off. There didn't seem to be any danger of Helena bothering to go to the trouble of usurping Sophie's place in Alana's affections. Now she had to do her best to ensure her niece was safe while she was in Helena's care.

* * *

Sophie was up even brighter and earlier than Alana the next morning, dressed, in full work mode and armed with several sheets of instructions she'd written up and printed out after her niece had gone to bed the night before.

Making a coffee, she then went to get Alana so she could give her her morning bottle before she left. Samson came downstairs, rather unkempt with his tousled hair. He wore pyjama bottoms, but no top. Sophie made sure she kept her eyes averted, especially when he came over to give Alana a tickle under her chin. At this point, she found herself involuntarily holding her breath, only letting it out when he left the room. He called out, "I'm going to hop in the shower. I'll give Helena a shout." This was becoming a habit she definitely needed to break.

Sophie heard the shower start, but Helena didn't show. The shower stopped. Sophie checked the clock on the microwave display; she needed to leave soon, and there wasn't any sign of Helena. There was no way she'd have a chance to go through all the notes she'd written now. Where was she? Helena knew both she and Samson had to leave early.

She fed a very grateful Mutt before Samson returned, dressed for work. Sophie hadn't seen him 'dressed up' before. Scrubbed and tailored he looked very good in his suit, his hair still damp, but combed back from his face so it didn't fall across his eyes as much as usual. He put his coffee cup in the sink.

"Sorry," he said. "Helena's coming, she's not much of a morning person. Do you need to go?"

"Kind of," admitted Sophie.

"It's OK, I'll take Alana. Helena will be down in a minute."

"I had notes . . ."

"Don't worry, I'll make sure Helena sees them." His voice dropped slightly in volume. "I programmed Alana's routine into her phone last night as well as a reminder to check in with me every hour so I know everything's going OK."

Sophie smiled at Samson's thoughtfulness. It was nice to know he was also a little concerned about how his girlfriend would cope alone with a baby for the day.

She kissed Alana, and handed her over to Samson, as Helena appeared in the doorway. She was gorgeous, as usual, but like she'd just crawled out of bed, complete with a pink sleep mask perched on the top of her head.

"You two look very cosy together," Helena commented, glaring at Sophie.

"I was just taking over with Alana until you came down," said Samson.

"Where's the coffee?" she snapped.

"I left you a cup by the side of the bed," Samson said.

"It went cold," came the reply as she walked past everyone to the kettle.

"Um, are you able to take Alana now? We both need to leave," asked Samson.

"Yeah, fine. Put her in her chair thing."

Sophie had to bite her lip to stop herself from saying that Alana wouldn't want to go in the highchair now, and if she did, there was no way she'd go in it again for her breakfast in half an hour. If she didn't leave right away, she'd be very late.

It took every ounce of will power she had to say as breezily as possible, "OK, I'll be off then, have a great day!" — and walk out of the front door.

* * *

Sophie's meeting went very well. The company knew her work from previously and were happy to take her on as a freelancer. There might be times when she'd need to visit their London offices, but basically, she could work from home doing whatever work they sent her. And she'd had a voice mail from the estate agents handling her flat letting her know they'd found tenants.

It was a big relief to have the security of some proper income coming in and not be surviving on tiny local jobs coming in dribs and drabs which was what she was suspecting she might have.

She even finished with them earlier than she'd expected. Pleased to be missing rush hour and able to get back to Alana, she hoped she might even have time to take her to the playground before tea.

Her mood rapidly changed though when she reached the front door of Samson's house and could hear Alana's screaming from the other side. She'd never heard her that incessant and distressed. What could have happened? Her heart beat faster as she fumbled frantically with her key in the lock, and rushed inside. She dumped her bag as she ran, following her niece's cries, up the stairs, along the hallway and to the baby's room. A very stressed Mutt was pawing at the door trying to get in. Sophie gently moved him out of the way and went in. Poor Alana was red in the face, crying her heart out and covered in milk sick. She smelt like she needed her nappy changed.

Sophie's ire towards Helena took a back seat as she comforted the baby. She picked her up and spoke softly to her, carrying her into the bathroom where she ran a warm bath with plenty of lavender baby bubble bath. Alana's little body, completely rigid with the effort of protesting her distress, gradually relaxed along with the volume of her cries. There was no point trying to keep the dog out of the room, he was resolute that he needed to stay with his new little sister.

By the time Alana was lifted from the bath and wrapped in a fluffy towel, the good-natured baby was smiling again but clung to her aunt in a way she didn't usually.

Sophie kept up ceaseless chitter-chatter to make Alana feel reassured, but once she had her clean and happy again, her anger returned. Where the hell was Helena? She knocked on Samson's bedroom and, when there was no answer, pushed open the door. The room was empty. The same was true of Samson's study.

She carried Alana downstairs to get her tea and see if there was any clue as to where Helena was.

They found her in the den, upside down against a wall with headphones on.

"Helena," said Sophie, as calmly as she could, then when she didn't get a response she shouted, "Helena!"

Helena's eyes opened and she gracefully climbed out of her pose. Only when she was on her feet and tightening her ponytail did she say, "Great, you're back." She picked up her yoga mat from the floor. "Tell Samson I'm going home to decompress," she continued, breezing past an astonished Sophie.

Helena had wafted into the kitchen before Sophie called out, "Alana was screaming her head off."

"Yeah," Helena answered from the next room. "I had to put on my headphones to block it out or I'd never have been able to focus on my mindfulness."

"How long did you leave her crying for?" Sophie questioned incredulously, now marching after Helena who clearly wasn't going to come to her.

"I don't know," huffed Helena, packing up her stuff into a Louis Vuitton handbag on the kitchen table. "She was all grisly, and it's not like there's a lot you can do with her other than feed her. Which, by the way, is gross."

"If you couldn't manage, you should have called Samson or me."

"It was fine."

"It was not fine," said Sophie in total exasperation. "Alana was very upset and covered with sick!"

"She seems OK now," said Helena.

"No thanks to you!"

Helena and Sophie glared at one another, each daring the other to continue.

"Is everything all right?" called Samson's voice as he came up the hallway. "The front door was wide open."

"Apparently I didn't do a good enough job looking after your daughter," said Helena haughtily before Sophie could get a word in.

Samson glanced from one woman to the other. "I'm sure Sophie wouldn't want you to feel like that . . ."

"Yes, I would actually," responded Sophie hotly.

"I don't have to take this! I was doing you a favour! I wasted the whole day dealing with a screaming kid! I'm going." Helena pushed past Samson and stormed out of the house.

A very confused Samson asked, "What's been going on? Why's Helena so upset?"

"You're worried about your irresponsible girlfriend?" Sophie said, disbelievingly. "What about Alana, your daughter?"

"Alana appears to be completely fine."

"Well, she wasn't. She was covered in vomit, wailing inconsolably and her nappy long-needed changing."

"I'm sure Helena did her best — she's not used to babies," he tried to placate.

"Neither were you until recently, but you coped!"

Samson ran his fingers through his hair. "I'd better go after her," he said.

"You do that!" Sophie turned away from him, furious. He clearly didn't believe her and was taking sides.

"We all need to try to get along here," he said calmly, obviously not wanting to leave Sophie when she was so angry. "None of us is perfect, and we're all going to do things a little differently . . ."

"She neglected your daughter and left her to cry so she could do her bloody yoga, Samson!"

"There are two sides to every story . . ."

"There's no other way of looking at this."

"I know you and Helena aren't exactly similar, and I've noticed you avoid her whenever possible . . ."

"What's that got to do with what she's done today?" asked Sophie slowly.

"Perhaps you're being a little hard on her . . ."

Sophie was too shocked to speak. She knew Samson was easy-going, but this was ridiculous. He couldn't genuinely think it was acceptable for Alana to have been treated the way she had been.

Finding her voice, she stated firmly, "Helena is not to look after Alana by herself."

"That's not a decision for you to make," Samson countered, softly, but with the same resolute expression on his face she'd seen after Natasha's funeral.

"We won't continue living here if Alana isn't safe."

"You're overreacting."

"No, I'm not."

They glared at one another, at a deadlock.

"I'm going after Helena. We'll speak more about this later," Samson said, leaving the house.

Sophie let out a sigh as the front door shut. Damn it! That hadn't gone well at all. Loyalty was a commendable attribute, but he was being plain unreasonable. She felt let down by Samson. Despite her first reservations, her gut instinct that he'd be useless and unreliable, when it came down to it, she'd come to trust and depend on him. Yes, and fancy him. But now this!

She was cleaning up Alana after her apple and pear dessert when her mobile buzzed with a text message from Samson. "Staying with Helena tonight, back tomorrow."

Though feeling like throwing the phone at the wall, Sophie put it down calmly. Screw him, she thought. If he was going to be like that, she and Alana were better off without him for the evening. At that moment, she wished they could be without him permanently.

CHAPTER 9

Sophie was still furious the following morning. No concrete plan had materialised over her night's 'sleep' and Sophie's conscious mind had very little to contribute. The best she had come up with so far was the old fall-back of avoiding Samson for as long as possible. She tried to rationalise that it was to give herself the greatest chance of calming down enough to argue her points reasonably when the 'discussion' resumed.

Her car was parked outside and she knew she could pack up the bare minimum and be out in less than an hour if she had to, but that wouldn't be the smartest move long-term. She and Samson had to be able to co-parent together, but Sophie wasn't prepared to give an inch regarding Helena being left alone with Alana again. She couldn't do anything about who Samson chose to date, but she should have a say in who cared for her niece. But how could she convince Samson she wasn't just being prejudiced against Helena? That she wasn't exaggerating and Samson's girlfriend had treated his daughter appallingly. It almost made her wish for one of those awful teddy bears she'd heard of, with cameras built in, to monitor nannies. Then Samson could have seen for himself exactly what had happened. That would prove she was telling the truth.

According to their schedule, Samson was due to be working away from the house. Unless he had a change of clothes at Helena's, she guessed he'd probably come home to shower and change before work, so she was up early and ready for the day. She didn't crave a confrontation right now, but wanted to be prepared. Arguing in your pyjamas was never a good look. But Samson didn't show.

Alana and Sophie went about their day together. Sophie had become very adept at fitting in setting up her new business around Alana. Nap times and evenings after her niece was in bed were her main work slots. It seemed to suit them both.

* * *

Sophie took Alana out for a stroll along the seafront and returned for the baby's afternoon nap. Samson's truck parked outside the house gave Sophie a head's up that he was back. She steeled herself before going in.

Alana was thrilled to see her father. She squealed in delight at the sight of him, bouncing up and down in her buggy until he released her from it, twirled her round in the air and enveloped her in a hug, to her huge delight.

Traitor, thought Sophie, though she had to admit they were very sweet together.

"It's time for Alana's sleep now, isn't it?" Samson asked politely.

"Yes, did you want to take her up?"

"If you don't mind, I'd love to. Why don't you put the kettle on? I need to talk to you if you've got time?"

"Of course," Sophie said, following his lead with overstated civility, though the last thing she wanted to do was hear excuses for Helena's behaviour again.

She went into the kitchen and made them both a cup of tea. Samson joined her as she finished. She handed him his mug and then sat opposite him at the table. Let the battle commence.

"I owe you an apology," he said immediately. "I was too quick to take Helena's side."

Sophie's heart leapt, but she managed to stay silent, waiting for him to continue.

"I guess I couldn't believe she'd be capable of treating Alana the way she did. It's incomprehensible she'd have so little patience, or that she wouldn't call me and ask for help if Alana was upset and she wasn't able to manage. But I should have supported you more. You love Alana and were upset, I should have listened to you. You wouldn't get carried away about something like that, I know."

"What made you change your mind?" Sophie asked.

"Helena's story about what happened didn't sit right last night when I was talking to her and trying to calm her down. The details kept changing. I couldn't sleep thinking about it, and then I had it out with her this morning."

"Wow," said Sophie quietly, relief flooding through her. She hadn't realised how tense and upset the fact Samson hadn't taken her seriously had made her, above and beyond her anger at Helena.

"She still doesn't see she's done anything wrong, but the little she's told me gave me enough to fill in the gaps. I won't have someone like that around Alana. We talked for a long time and it was clear she doesn't see Alana as becoming a major part of her life, so . . . we broke up."

"Oh," Sophie said, unsure of what else to say. She didn't want Samson to think she was completely unsympathetic if he was upset, but at the same time, she couldn't help but be happy about the turn of events. "Are you all right?"

"I think so," he admitted. "We were never particularly well-suited to be honest, and it had to be done. We couldn't have a future together with her not willing to fully include Alana in that. I ought to have spoken to Helena properly about things before, about how Alana would affect us, but I was putting it off, hoping she'd get used to Alana, and some buried maternal instinct would kick in."

"Alana is pretty adorable — it wasn't a completely stupid idea . . ."

"Well, it didn't work, but at least I know now. And I am so sorry my . . . experiment backfired on you and Alana. I didn't think for one moment anything bad would happen. It must have been horrible for you to come home to find Alana so upset."

"It was," admitted Sophie. "I can't comprehend how Helena could leave her like that."

Samson shook his head as if trying to rid his mind of the thought.

"And then when I tried to tell you what had happened, and you took Helena's side . . ."

"That was terrible of me," he said sincerely. He got up and walked around the table. "Come here," he said, taking her hand. Sophie stood up, and Samson drew her into a hug. Sophie was taken a little by surprise, and her heart started beating double time at his proximity.

"This has all been a huge change for us, and it's going to be tough at times. But you and I, we have to be a team. Team Alana," he said gently.

Sophie struggled to contain tears of relief which threatened to pour down her face. She was so glad Helena was now out of the picture. Samson's words had acted to reassure her that he saw her as a partner in bringing up her niece, and respected her.

"I need to make a couple of phone calls, but I'll get Alana up from her nap at four. I thought I'd take her to the supermarket with me," said Samson.

"She'll like that."

"I was going to make some seriously delicious salmon for dinner if you'll join me?"

Seeing Sophie hesitate, he continued, "It's ridiculous us eating separately, and, let's face it, you admitted yourself that you're a terrible cook."

Sophie laughed — she was certainly tempted.

"I'll get something for pudding . . ." Samson offered.

"Fine!" Sophie cried, her self-constraint broken. "I'll have dinner with you."

"Have you got work stuff you need to catch up on?"

"I've got a couple of emails I should reply to."

"Do you want to come to the supermarket with Alana and me anyway? We could walk, it's a nice evening. Maybe you could show me the park you take her to? I'd love to see her on the swings."

"Sure." Sophie smiled, so relieved to have things back on an even keel between them. At that moment she wanted nothing more than to spend a relaxing few hours with Samson and Alana.

* * *

Samson began cooking while Sophie finished putting Alana to bed. Sophie then went into her room to brush her hair and reapply the little bit of make-up she had on. She wanted to put on some mascara as well, and ideally change her outfit. She realised she wanted Samson to think she looked nice and chastised herself: the poor guy had only just broken up with his girlfriend. She should be commiserating with him, not thinking about making herself more attractive to get his attention. And more importantly, she and Samson were still very much finding their way when it came to working together to bring up Alana. Helena had thrown a major spanner in the works of that, but, hopefully, with her no longer around, they could get back on track. Their relationship was already more than complicated enough without adding romance into the equation. And was it weird of her to be attracted to Natasha's ex, even if the two of them hadn't been together very long? How would she compare to her beautiful, fun and up-for-anything older sister, who'd always been the life and soul of the party? Did Samson see her as ugly and boring by comparison?

What was the point in pondering these things, she asked herself firmly. It wouldn't be sensible for her and Samson to rock the boat of their newly re-established friendship, too much was at stake. And anyway, the likelihood of Samson being attracted to her after being with Natasha and Helena was minuscule — they were in a completely different league to her. She should focus on enjoying the evening and rejoice that that awful Helena was now well and truly out of the picture.

The food was already smelling mouthwatering as she came downstairs to join Samson. She grinned, remembering how excited Samson was to see Alana on the swings, and how he'd filmed it and then showed the video to the checkout lady at the supermarket.

He'd insisted on carrying the shopping home, and it had been nice to feel looked after, Sophie realised. It had been a very long time since she had been. And was it her imagination, or did they all, not only her, seem more relaxed now Helena was out of the picture?

A glass of wine was poured ready for her.

"Yum," Sophie said, taking a sip.

Samson passed her a terracotta bowl filled with herby olives.

"I could get used to this," she said happily, helping herself to one.

"Alana settled quickly for you," Samson commented.

"I think we must have worn her out."

Sophie drank another sip of wine before asking, "So, how are you really doing about Helena?"

"I'm good I think," he said, to Sophie's relief. "I could never be with someone who wasn't prepared to fully take on Alana as well as me. She's the most important thing in my life now."

"In fairness to Helena, she didn't know she'd be taking on Alana when she started dating you."

"Yeah, I get that. I was a very different person when I met Helena, but Alana's here now, and she's not going anywhere."

"I'm sorry it didn't work out for you guys."

"No, you're not," Samson said, with a knowing smile.

"Fair enough." Sophie pulled a face. "I'm not. She was horrible."

"Turns out she was," admitted Samson.

Samson served pan-fried salmon with sauté potatoes and steamed tenderstem broccoli and mange tout. It was completely delicious. As was the apple crumble and custard he produced for pudding.

The combination of the relief of having Helena gone and the alcohol, made Sophie feel more relaxed with Samson than she ever had before.

"So . . ." began Samson awkwardly, as they cleared the table and loaded the dishwasher. "My mum and dad are pretty desperate to meet Alana . . ."

"Of course they are! Are you going to take her to visit them? Where do they live?"

"Yeah, I was hoping to this weekend. Their house is near Oxford, so not too far. My sisters are going to be there as well."

"How many sisters have you got?"

"Two, Bethan and Maria. They're both older than me. They basically spent my teenage years chasing girls away from me so I could concentrate on my schoolwork."

"I'm sure you were very grateful," she said, laughing.

"Not at the time." Samson grimaced.

"Is Alana your mum and dad's first grandchild?"

"Yeah."

Samson's short response made Sophie wonder if he wanted the subject closed, but then he continued, "It was a bit of a shock when I told them, but they're so excited about meeting her. They loved the video of her on the swing. My mum's been watching it non-stop since I sent it to them."

"How long will you and Alana be away for?" Sophie asked. Now she was wondering what she'd do with herself for a whole weekend without her niece in the house. Maybe she could visit some of her friends in London. She'd been very remiss about keeping in touch with them since Natasha had passed away . . . but they'd want to go out to a club or something and she really wasn't sure she was ready for that yet. Her cheerful mood had definitely gone down a notch.

"I was thinking of leaving Saturday morning and coming back Sunday evening. That way it's only one night away from home for Alana."

"Sounds like a good plan."

"Actually . . . I was wondering if you'd come with us?" Samson asked tentatively.

"Me? Why?" Sophie asked in surprise.

"I thought Alana would like it . . ." explained Samson, lamely, and not quite meeting her eye.

Sophie was sceptical. "Is that the real reason?"

"No," Samson admitted. "Though it would be nice for Alana if you came. And for me."

"You're nervous, aren't you?"

"Maybe a bit. I've never been in sole charge of Alana for a night by myself, and she's going to be in a house she's not used to," he said sheepishly.

"Why would you be nervous, it's only your family?"

"There are rather a lot of them."

"And . . ."

"And they've never seen me with a baby before."

"You're worried she's going to be difficult and cry all the time?" asked Sophie, struggling not to laugh.

"Maybe a bit," he admitted. "She'll be happier with you there."

Sophie smiled at his confession. She'd often felt like she struggled so much more with Alana than he did, him being so confident and a natural with her. It was nice to hear he wanted her help.

"Won't your mum and dad mind?"

"I've told them all about you. They want to meet you and would love you to come. I guess you're the closest they'll get to knowing Alana's mother."

"Sure," said Sophie, feeling a poor second to her sister all of a sudden.

"My mum thinks it's wonderful how you dropped everything and stepped up for Alana when Natasha died."

"She's more than worth it." Sophie's spirits lifted a little.

The cleaning-up was finished, and Sophie had already spent far longer wiping down the kitchen surfaces than was strictly necessary. "Well, thanks for a lovely supper," she said, "I'll head upstairs now. See you in the morning."

Samson looked like he was wanting to say something, but changed his mind, and nodded. "Sleep well," he called out as she left.

* * *

Sophie, Samson, Mutt and Alana were ready to leave after breakfast on Saturday. Samson seemed even more nervous than Sophie as they packed up her car. Once the dog, Alana, her bags, travel cot and buggy were in there, there wasn't a lot of space for anything else. Sophie had to put her overnight bag by her feet. Samson was driving as he knew the way.

Samson's family lived in a village outside Oxford, a two-hour trip. Traffic permitting, they were hoping to get there without having to stop on the way.

They drove out of Brighton. Alana fell asleep quickly and they listened to the radio. Samson told Sophie more about his work, and some of the projects he'd been involved in — she was impressed. It seemed he played down how good he was at his job. She couldn't help thinking back to her first impression of him when she opened Natasha's front door and saw him for the first time. He was nothing like the lazy, surfer dude she'd envisaged. She found it hard to imagine Samson and her sister together; they didn't exactly seem well-suited.

They arrived at Samson's parents' picture-perfect village, complete with cricket green, country pub and duck pond, and continued up a narrow country lane for another kilometre or so, then pulled up outside the gates of an old vicarage, set inside ancient-looking stone walls, covered in a cloak of ivy and honeysuckle.

"This is where you were brought up?" Sophie asked incredulously.

"Yep," answered Samson, climbing out of the car.

Yikes, thought Sophie. This was exactly the type of house she would have loved to have grown up in. It was like something from an Enid Blyton novel with its sash windows and red brick facade.

The front door was flung open and a small, round woman with long grey hair and wearing a bright orange flowing top and loose, pale linen trousers, came hurrying out and straight over to Samson, enveloping him in a hug.

"Hi, Mum, it's good to see you," Samson said, affectionately, hugging her back.

"Where is she?" she asked excitedly, pulling away from Samson and peering around him to the car.

Smiling, Samson opened the car's back door. He reached in, undid Alana's seatbelt and brought the baby out, handing her to her grandmother.

Glancing back at the house, Sophie saw a large man, probably in his sixties, standing in the doorway.

"Hey, Dad," said Samson, noticing him, "Come and meet Alana."

Samson definitely took after his father with his looks, except for his mouth and eyes, Sophie noticed, which were like his mother's.

His father came to join his wife, and she passed him Alana.

"Mum, Dad, this is Sophie," Samson introduced, once the initial excitement of his parents holding their grandchild for the first time had calmed.

"Hi," she said, giving a self-conscious little wave.

Samson's mum gave Sophie a hug. "It's so good to meet you. I'm Maggie, and this is my husband, Peter."

Peter removed his focus from his granddaughter briefly to smile a welcome.

"Come inside," ushered Maggie, and she and Peter walked together towards the house, both cooing over the baby, Mutt close at their heels, eager not to miss out on any of the action.

Sophie followed hesitantly. This was a very private family moment, and she felt she was intruding. She wished she'd stayed behind in Brighton, but then she'd be alone in Samson's home for the weekend. For the first time since she left it, Sophie missed her little London flat. She longed for somewhere that was hers which she could hide away in.

She faltered outside the door, debating. Despite Samson's plea for her to come, should she offer to stay at a hotel and leave the family to themselves — would they be grateful not to have the outsider hanging around, or insulted that she wouldn't be sleeping in their home? As if sensing her doubt, Samson turned and gave her a reassuring smile. He held out his hand, and Sophie accepted it.

"Don't worry, they're not nearly as scary as they seem," he joked, leading her into the house.

Sophie's awkwardness was eased further when they reached the large country-style kitchen, and Maggie's welcoming warmth couldn't help but make her relax.

"You must both be tired after your drive," Maggie said. "Why don't you take your things up to your rooms and have a wash up while I get a pot of tea on?" she suggested. "I wasn't sure where you'd like Alana to sleep, so put the travel cot wherever you think is best."

Sophie and Samson went upstairs, leaving Alana with her grandparents. He was in his old bedroom, which Sophie didn't get a chance to get a decent peek at before he led her up another level to the attic bedroom she'd be sleeping in.

"I'm happy to have Alana in with me if you like," Sophie offered.

"Sure," Samson replied easily. "I'll set up her cot at the bottom of the bed."

Samson going out to the car to retrieve the travel cot he'd bought for the occasion, gave Sophie time to properly examine her surroundings. The large window facing the bed looked out over the walled garden. The oak furniture was antique, though well-loved and a bit battered on the edges. Thick cream carpet covered the floor and the wall was papered in a floral Laura Ashley print. Sophie wondered whether this room had previously belonged to one or both of Samson's sisters.

Samson was soon back, setting up the cot and then the baby monitor while Sophie put the sheets and blankets in the cot ready for Alana's nap.

"I don't know who's happier down there, Mum or Alana," he commented.

"We'd better get lunch into Alana soon," Sophie said, "or she won't stay happy for long."

"Good point!" Samson laughed.

They went back downstairs to the kitchen to discover Alana being doted upon, adoringly.

"Would you both like a cup of tea, and then I'll get us some lunch?" asked Maggie.

"Sounds great, Mum." Samson put his arm around her shoulders and squeezed her affectionately. Sophie wondered if Maggie was feeling as nervous as she was; it was certainly a very strange situation Maggie found herself in. How often does your son bring his newly discovered daughter and her aunt to stay?

"Do you mind if I give Alana her lunch now?" Sophie asked.

"Of course!" said Maggie. "Can I do anything to help?"

"Well . . . would you like to feed her? Be warned — it can get quite messy."

"I'd love to!"

Samson attached a portable little seat he'd bought for Alana the day before to one of the kitchen chairs and popped her in while Sophie got out a jar of Alana's favourite food, her spoon, a bib, and her beaker of water.

Alana made short work of her meal much to her grand-parents' delight and was thrilled when she received applause for drinking out of her beaker by herself. The smiles were wide and enthusiastic all round.

Sophie and Samson sipped their teas, catching each other's eye now and again when Alana did something particularly endearing.

The star of the show was cleaned up with wet wipes and cheerfully gnawed on rice cakes while the adults tucked into a delicious Salade Nicoise.

While Alana napped, Sophie was given a tour of the garden by Peter, and then when the baby woke, they all set out for a walk around the village. Maggie pushed Alana's buggy proudly. There was a playground in the corner of the village green which they took Alana to. She loved going down the toddler slide on her daddy's lap and all the grown-ups were in stitches laughing at Samson getting wedged at the top.

Sophie spent a lot of the time watching the others and their family dynamic. Samson was obviously much-loved by both his parents, and it was very sweet to see how supportive they were of him.

She had vague memories of similar times with her own parents and grandparents, and Natasha of course. Not necessarily big events but just having fun and being with family.

Naturally, whenever they'd been at a playground, Natasha was always the child who swung highest on the swings, went down the slide backwards and climbed to the very top of the rigging, encouraging Sophie, who was more inclined to caution.

Supper for the grown-ups was lasagne and salad after Alana had been put to bed. It was a while before Alana would settle in the unusual room and cot. Sophie played sous-chef for Maggie while poor Samson went up and down the stairs, comforting his daughter until she finally fell asleep after an hour.

* * *

"He's very good with Alana, isn't he?" Maggie commented to Sophie as they loaded the dishwasher together once everyone had finished eating, and Peter and Samson walked Mutt through the fields at the back of the house.

"He really is," agreed Sophie.

"It's come as a shock. A lovely shock though," she added quickly. "I can't believe my baby has a baby. She's so gorgeous."

"Yes, she is."

"It must have been very hard for you, your sister dying so suddenly."

"It was." Sophie took a moment to get her emotions under control after the mention of Natasha. "But Alana helps," she managed to continue. "I feel like I've still got part of my sister with me."

Maggie drew Sophie into her arms.

"Thank you," Maggie said. "Thank you for everything you're doing. Samson told us how supportive you've been, how you've helped him, taught him how to look after Alana."

"I'm not sure he was the one who needed help," said Sophie honestly. Feeling embarrassed, she returned to her job.

"That's not what he told us."

Samson appeared at the kitchen doorway holding a Scrabble board hopefully. "Anyone for a game?"

"Sure," said Sophie.

"As long as you don't make up any words!" Maggie replied.

"I don't make up words!" he said indignantly.

"Yes, you do. Just because you can find them on the internet does not make them real words you can use in Scrabble. Only words from the official Scrabble dictionary we bought you for Christmas ten years ago and you've never used, will be allowed."

"Fine, I'll still beat you," Samson said cheerfully.

They sat around the kitchen table playing. Maggie was right: Samson did try to invent words — but they ganged up on him so he didn't get to use them. He still won by a landslide though.

"Last time I beat him, Samson was about twelve," Peter admitted. "His sisters refuse to play with him."

"They're sore losers," Samson declared.

"I dare you to say that to their faces!" Peter joked. He turned to Sophie. "Those two know how to keep this troublemaker in line."

"They're both coming for lunch tomorrow," Maggie commented. "They can't wait to meet their niece."

"Are the guys coming?" Samson asked.

"Yes," said Maggie happily. "They'll all be here around one."

"Bethan's married to Ed, they live in London," Samson explained, "and Maria and her boyfriend, Ryan, are coming from Bristol. They work at the university there."

"Maria's a researcher in the physics department," said Peter proudly, putting the kettle on. "Cup of tea anyone?"

Sophie tried to stifle a yawn as best as she could; Alana had had her up early, and the day was catching up with her now.

"Would anyone mind if I turned in?" she asked.

"Of course not," Maggie said understandingly. "Let us know if there's anything you need. We'll see you in the morning." She got up and gave Sophie a good night hug. "Thank you so much for coming. It's lovely to have you here," she said quietly.

* * *

Sophie groaned when she was woken by Alana stirring at seven the next morning. The baby had been restless sleeping in a different house and Sophie had ended up giving her a bottle at 3 a.m. to settle her. Sophie was tired but knew she'd better get the little girl up straight away though; she didn't want her disturbing everyone if they wanted to sleep in a bit. She was hauling herself out of bed when there was a quiet knock at her bedroom door.

"Sophie, it's me, Samson. Would you like me to take Alana for you?"

Sophie opened the door to him. "Are you sure you don't mind?"

"Nah, I was getting up anyway. You grab some extra kip."

Alana went happily to her dad, and Sophie settled back into bed for another hour before having a long, hot bath and heading downstairs to join the family for breakfast.

Peter was sitting at the kitchen table watching the news on the little television in the corner of the room. "Morning," he said pleasantly. "Maggie's outside doing some gardening and Samson's taken Alana and Mutt to get the paper and some fresh bread — they'll be back soon. Help yourself to tea or there's fresh coffee in the pot."

"Thanks." Sophie felt a bit shy being by herself with Samson's father.

She poured herself a coffee and went through the open French doors into the garden. Maggie was giving everything a water with the hose before it got hot.

"Good morning! Did you sleep well?" Maggie asked cheerfully. Ah, a morning person.

"Yes, thank you."

"Did Alana sleep through?"

"I had to give her a feed during the night, but then she settled. She usually sleeps right through."

"She's a good baby, isn't she? Samson didn't sleep through for me until he was nearly two!"

"You must have been exhausted!"

"Just a bit. Some days I must have looked like a zombie dropping the girls off at school. By the time we got back, Samson would have fallen asleep and wouldn't wake up for a good couple of hours! It would drive me crazy, but he was always such a happy baby, you couldn't be cross with him for long."

"We're back!" Samson called from inside the house. Maggie and Sophie went to greet him. Alana was being carried by Samson but she held out her arms when she saw Sophie approaching. Sophie took her and the baby snuggled into her, the greatest feeling in the world.

"Toast, all?" Samson asked, holding up a loaf of fresh bread.

Everyone answered in the affirmative, including Mutt if the frantic wagging of his tail was anything to go by, and Samson set about making them all toast with butter and jam, which proved very popular with Alana.

"Right," said Maggie, "I've got a big Sunday roast to cook. You toddle off and have fun. Make sure you're back by one!"

"Let's take Alana out for a few hours," declared Samson. "Dad, do you want to come?"

"I think I'm on potato-peeling duty," Peter replied stoically.

"Sophie?"

"Sure, that would be good," she replied, feeling unexpected excitement bubbling inside her.

"Get yourself ready, I'll sort out a bottle to take along for Alana. The changing bag is all packed, will she need anything else?"

"That sounds like everything," Sophie said happily. It was lovely to feel valued by Samson and to be treated like she was important and knew what she was doing, even though she still felt like she was winging it with Alana most of the time.

* * *

A short while later, and Samson, Sophie, Mutt and Alana were in Sophie's car heading towards Hinksey Park, a favourite of Samson's from his childhood.

They pushed Alana in her buggy around the park while Mutt trotted alongside on his lead, but in her opinion, the best thing was to sit on a bench by the lake and giggle at the swans and the model boats. Samson and Sophie sat on either side of her, both being extra vigilant in case the baby suddenly decided to throw herself off the bench in an effort to get at some of the mesmerising things she was watching.

The little girl was so fascinated with the birds, Samson picked her up to get a better view. Sophie pulled out her mobile and snapped a photo of the two of them. She was checking it and contemplating taking another shot when Samson carried Alana over to her to have a look. An elderly couple walked by with a little terrier who Mutt immediately made friends with. The woman stopped and commented lightly, "You have a very beautiful family."

"Thank you," Samson replied, simply.

Sophie raised an eyebrow at him once the people were out of sight.

"What?" he said, shrugging. "Did you want to go into the whole story with them?"

"Fair point," Sophie agreed. She was filled with a warm glow at being so easily mistaken for a family, and at Samson's reaction to it. Could it be that he also felt she and him becoming closer? That he felt at least part of the attraction she did for him? It was certainly beginning to feel like he might. He was attentive to her and seemed to be actively seeking out her company. Sophie was also sure he was more tactile than previously, touching her hand to get her attention or brushing a stray eyelash from her cheek.

They left the park in search of a coffee shop and were soon settled at a table outside with a couple of Americanos, which they drank while Sophie gave Alana her bottle. Checking the time when they'd finished, they realised they needed to head back or they'd be in trouble with Maggie.

* * *

The few hours out with Alana and Samson had been fun, and things had felt so comfortable, that Sophie hadn't thought much about meeting Samson's sisters. But when they arrived back at his parents' house and spotted the extra cars outside, she began to feel very nervous. She thought she'd done pretty well with Samson's family so far — was it pushing her luck trying to win over four more members? It was all so strange. She felt like she was meeting a boyfriend's family for the first time, judging and being judged, worried she was being assessed for suitability. Of course, all of that was true in a way, and even possibly more so bearing in mind she was their granddaughter's mother figure, a fixed addition to their closest circle.

But she soon realised she needn't have worried. They entered the house and could hear everyone chatting in the kitchen. The whole family seemed to turn as one when they came in. Samson's sisters were very similar, both younger versions of their mother. They came over to greet Sophie and Alana with big smiles on their faces, hugging Sophie and welcoming her. They then crowded around Samson and fussed over the baby who was happy to be handed over while their partners introduced themselves to Sophie.

Sophie thought to herself how lovely it was that Alana was so content to go to her aunts, but she also felt a pang of jealousy. As Alana's aunts they had exactly the same familial relationship with her precious niece as she did. Suddenly her own relationship with Alana seemed a little precarious, and perhaps not as special as she'd come to think of it as. She told herself sternly to stop being ridiculous. She was having a lovely day but was in danger of spoiling it by focusing on her private feelings of inadequacy.

Samson's sisters were clearly used to seeing him as the baby of the family, which Sophie found amusing to observe.

He was far taller than either of them, and in his thirties, but they continued to tease him like the younger brother he was.

Sophie had always wanted more siblings, especially once Natasha had reached teenagerhood and wanted absolutely nothing to do with her annoying younger sister. Mealtimes then tended to be just Sophie and her mum and dad; Natasha would either be out with her friends or, more often, would have stormed off to her room after arguing with her parents. The three of them would eat their food in near silence, Sophie's mother trying not to cry, and her father making occasional attempts at conversation now and again attempting to cheer them up. Eventually, they gave up trying to eat as a family, and even when Natasha left home at sixteen, to everyone's relief if she were truly honest, they never resumed the practice, and Sophie soon became very adept at heating things up for herself in the microwave.

Things could not have been more different in this household. Maggie and Peter began piling dishes of food on the table: roast beef, huge, fluffy Yorkshire puddings, crisp roast potatoes, stuffing, gravy, carrots, broccoli and runner beans. Maria and Bethan laid the table, and Samson poured drinks for everyone. Sophie suspected these had been their jobs at mealtimes for as long as any of them could remember.

Sophie had never experienced anything like the busy, family meal which ensued. Nine people squeezed around a kitchen table, several conversations going on at once, dishes being passed around . . . it was all very new and different. It felt like something she'd see in a film. Alana had had a nap in the car as they drove back from the park so she was in great spirits and loved trying some different foods and watching everyone. She seemed to fit in easily with this family dynamic. Sophie wasn't sure the same could perhaps be said of herself: she'd tried but felt a little out of her comfort zone. Overwhelmed, she retreated into herself and spent the meal listening to what everyone else was saying.

A jolt shot through her as she felt Samson's hand on her arm. She turned to him. "Are you OK?" he asked gently. "You're very quiet."

"I'm fine," she said, smiling. It was sweet he'd checked on her.

"Don't worry," said Bethan's husband, Ed. "You'll soon get used to this noisy lot."

"Of course she will," said Maggie kindly, patting Sophie's hand. "In time you go a little deaf which definitely helps!"

Sophie felt herself beginning to unwind — it was lovely to think she'd be seeing this family again. They'd been so welcoming, and, while she didn't feel properly part of it yet, she relished the thought that she could work towards that.

CHAPTER 10

Back in Brighton the next day, Sophie and Samson decided to take it in turns to catch up with work while Alana was awake, but first Samson watched Alana so Sophie could have her shower. He told her not to hurry, that he needed to sort the office out a bit before he could start work anyway and Alana could help.

The door to Samson's office was closed when she was finished and went to collect Alana. She knocked, not wanting to push open the door in case Alana was behind it.

"Just a minute!" came the reply.

Sophie waited. What on earth was happening on the other side of the door? She could hear all sorts of noises. It sounded like a major refurb was going on, not a quick tidy up.

"Is everything all right in there?" she asked eventually, curious, but mainly fed up of waiting.

"Almost done!" called back Samson. "Go and make us both a cup of tea and I'll be finished."

Sophie thumped downstairs. Why couldn't he pass Alana out to her if he was busy?

While the kettle boiled, she saw she had a missed call from Yvonne, the social worker, and took the opportunity to call her back so she could fill her in on how things were going. Yvonne definitely seemed surprised to hear Sophie and Alana were now living with Alana's father. "How did that come about?" she asked.

Sophie filled her in on the details of their arrangement.

"How's it working out?" Yvonne asked cautiously.

"We definitely had a few kinks that needed ironing out to begin with, but I think we're doing pretty well now."

"Would it be all right if I came by to meet Samson and check how Alana's doing?" Yvonne asked.

"Sure."

"Would this afternoon at around four be convenient?"

"Oh . . . um . . . yes I think so. Yes, that would be fine," said Sophie, mentally tallying up what she'd need to do to get the house ready with this very short notice.

"Marvellous."

"Right. Well, we'll see you then."

When Sophie returned upstairs with a cup of tea in each hand a few minutes later, the office door was still closed. Sighing to herself, she banged on the door with her elbow. Finally, it was opened by Samson who had Alana in his arms. "Ta-da!"

He stepped back to reveal a cleared table. Sophie recalled it had been next to Samson's main desk with a printer and general clutter on it. Now it was opposite where he worked. Perched on top was a cardboard sign with 'Sophie Perring' scrawled on it.

"This is for me?" Sophie asked.

"I thought it would be more comfortable for you than using your laptop on your bed, and less distracting than the kitchen table."

"Wow! It's brilliant!" Sophie put the mugs down on her new desk and gave Samson and Alana a hug. "Thank you both very much. It's very thoughtful of you. It will be so good to have somewhere I can spread out my work and not have to worry about cleaning it up all the time."

"To be honest, it was all me," Samson said. "Alana was frankly no help at all. It turns out she's rubbish at moving around furniture."

"Well, thank you then," said Sophie. "Let me take Trouble for a while so you can get started on work. We can swap in a couple of hours."

"Nah, you have the first turn. I can send a few emails from my phone while I watch her. Get it set up as you'd like, and then you can tell me if there's anything you need or you want me to change around."

"OK, thanks. Oh, I spoke to the social worker who's been assigned to Alana while I was downstairs. She'd like to come to meet you and see Alana later, at four," Sophie said, suddenly wondering if she should have checked with Samson before making the appointment. She knew he was planning to be at home, but it was his house. Was it all right for her to invite anyone over without checking first? "Sorry, I should have asked you first . . ."

"Don't be daft, it's fine. Should I be scared though?" Samson asked.

"No, she's lovely, but I should probably have a tidy round . . ."

"I'll make a start downstairs now."

"Seriously?"

"Of course, we want the place nice when this woman comes. Team Alana, remember?"

"That would be amazing. I'll take over at eleven?"

"Right ho, see you in a bit then. Shout if you want a coffee and help yourself to anything you need in here."

Sophie brought her laptop and paperwork through to the office and set up her desk. It might be a bit weird being directly in front of Samson if they were both working in there, but that was something she'd have to get used to. It would be much easier for her to concentrate with a proper base, and so thoughtful of Samson to give up some more of his space for her. He'd turned out to be so, so different to what she'd assumed. He was kind, decent and tried his very best for Alana. And despite their rocky start, with everything he'd done and did every day for her, she felt like he was making room in his home and life for them both.

When she had the security of her guardianship being made official, they could hash out the details of a permanent arrangement to bring up Alana together.

* * *

The doorbell rang soon after four while Sophie was changing Alana's nappy, and she heard Samson greet Yvonne. By the time Sophie and her niece came downstairs, it was clear Samson had well and truly charmed Yvonne. They were sat in the garden like two old friends enjoying a catch-up over a cuppa.

"Sophie! Hello again," said Yvonne, warmly. "And Alana, how are you, sweetheart?"

She was rewarded with one of the baby's most endearing smiles.

"Samson's been filling me in on Alana. It sounds like things are going well," Yvonne said, checking her notes.

"Yes," said Sophie, sitting down to join them. "It's certainly much easier looking after a baby when you've got another adult around."

"Now, Samson, your name isn't on Alana's birth certificate . . ." confirmed Yvonne.

"No," Samson said. "I was only told about her the day before her mother died."

Sophie felt a rush of sympathy for him being questioned by a stranger about this very painful subject.

"I see . . ." continued the social worker. "That does make things rather complicated. You had no relationship with your daughter until very recently, and there's no proof you are her father as yet. I suppose the first thing to do would be to organise a paternity test."

"I'm happy to do that," said Samson.

"Are you planning to apply for joint parental custody?" Yvonne asked.

"We haven't discussed it," Sophie replied.

"I guess so, it seems like the most sensible thing to do," said Samson, glancing over at Sophie. "I haven't felt the need to rush anything. Everything's going so well and we're all settling into our new lives."

"Is that something that needs to be decided now?" said Sophie.

"No, not at all, just something to think about. The important thing is Alana seems happy and is obviously thriving."

"She is."

"And I understand you went to visit Samson's family at the weekend?"

"Yes, near Oxford."

"So, quite the support network now, which is nice to see. It's still very early days," Yvonne continued, "but I'm very pleased with how things are panning out here. Alana's a lucky little girl."

"Thank you," said Sophie and Samson together.

The visit finished with a tour of the house, and an agreement that Yvonne would come again in a month.

Sophie was glad when the social worker had gone. She'd been very pleasant, but some of her questions had been awkward to say the least, especially when she said Samson's situation was difficult as he'd only known about Alana for such a short time. Sophie knew it was imperative no one find out that she was in exactly the same position herself. She couldn't let anything weaken her claim to guardianship of Alana.

"Are you all right?" she asked Samson once she'd seen Yvonne drive off.

"Yeah," he said. "How do you reckon that went?"

"Fine. I think she liked you," Sophie teased. "She certainly seemed much more interested in talking to you than me."

"That's only because she'd already met you. She knows you're not a complete imbecile."

"Anyone who sees you and Alana together knows you're a great dad."

"Thank you. It's a bit disconcerting knowing she's checking if you're safe to look after your baby."

"It is," agreed Sophie. "But she said she thought everything was good here."

"What are your plans for the rest of the afternoon? Do you want to take Alana out somewhere to celebrate the visit going well?"

"Sure. Actually, it's my twenty-eighth birthday today," admitted Sophie.

Samson looked taken aback. "Your birthday? Why didn't you say?"

She smiled. "I'm saying now!"

"But I haven't even got you a card!"

"Don't worry, I never make a big deal of my birthday."

"Well, we are this year. Alana and I are taking you out for supper."

"You don't have to!" Sophie said quickly, though she so hoped Samson wouldn't change his mind. She loved the idea of going to a restaurant to celebrate.

"Absolutely. I'll book a table somewhere. Better make it early for Alana. Six thirty?"

"OK, thank you!"

"I'll have Alana, you spend some time on yourself. Be ready to leave at six fifteen."

"Brilliant!" Sophie said, excited at the thought of being treated.

She managed to get herself a last-minute appointment with a hairdresser close by. It was lovely to be heading out to do something for herself.

She returned at six, her hair trimmed and layered, her nails manicured, and with a new dress.

She called out "Hello?" and received a reply from Samson's study. "I'll be out in a bit!"

Sophie went into her bedroom to do her make-up and put on her new dress. It was much more feminine than her usual choice of outfit: a pink floral tea dress which she teamed with some white ballet slippers. The outfit had seemed like a good idea in the shop. She stared at herself judgementally in the mirror — did she look silly? Like she'd made too much of an effort? What if they were going to Pizza Hut? She'd feel ridiculous.

She was about to change, when she heard Samson holler up the stairs, "Are you ready?"

There was no time to swap her outfit for some jeans and a top now; she'd have to go as she was.

Samson and Alana were waiting for her by the front door. Mutt sat hopefully next to them — Alana was strapped into her buggy, and he knew that meant 'walkies'.

Samson had changed into a blue short-sleeved cotton shirt and chinos and he'd put Alana into a pretty yellow party dress with butterflies on and attempted to style her hair in bunches.

"Wow," he said as Sophie came into view. "You look amazing."

"Thank you," she said, blushing. "You don't think it's too much?"

"It's just enough," Samson replied. "Did you change your hair?"

"Yeah, I went to the hairdressers this afternoon."

"It suits you," he commented.

"I considered dyeing it as well, but I wasn't brave enough," she confessed.

"I like your natural colour," said Samson, with a shrug.

"I think I've always seen it as a bit dull and longed for Natasha's thick, blonde hair. I guess I thought it would make me more exciting and glamorous, more technicolour like Natasha, and less black and white."

"You are not black and white," said Samson, softly.

"Well, thank you." Sophie was embarrassed to have been so honest, but her tummy fluttered in response to Samson's reply. "Shall we get going?" she suggested, wanting to change the topic of conversation.

"Absolutely," agreed Samson. "I thought we'd walk as it's such a nice evening. It's not far. Mutt, I'm afraid you're staying here, but I'll see what I can do about bringing home a doggy bag."

Mutt was most aggrieved and plonked himself dejectedly at the bottom of the stairs, too affronted for the comfort of his basket.

They walked towards the city centre with Samson commenting on some of the architecture around them then turned down a side street Sophie hadn't noticed before on her own wanderings. Tucked away was a tiny Italian restaurant.

"It's not the swankiest of places, but the food is fantastic and I've been coming here for years," Samson explained.

Samson was greeted cheerfully by the rather rotund owner who he introduced to Sophie as Francesco and all the staff were called over to fuss over Alana. A highchair and grissini were found for her, and glasses of Chianti were poured.

"You are a lucky man having supper with two beautiful ladies," commented Francesco to Samson when he brought over a plate of antipasti.

"I am indeed." Samson smiled at Sophie.

Francesco left them, and Samson pulled an envelope out of the changing bag hanging on the back of Alana's buggy.

"Alana and I made you this," he said, presenting it to Sophie.

She opened the envelope to find a card inside with Alana's footprints on the front in blue paint.

"It's lovely," said Sophie. "How on earth did you get her to sit still for long enough to make it?"

"I didn't . . . there's rather a lot of blue paint still on my desk and her feet," he admitted. "And there's this," said Samson, handing Sophie a small package. Inside was a white gold chain with a locket. "Open it," he urged.

Sophie pried it open. There was a lock of Alana's hair tucked inside.

"Thank you!" Sophie exclaimed. "It's beautiful. How did you have time to organise this?"

"We snuck out while you were at the hairdresser. I was trying to cut the piece of hair to go in it when you arrived back. Shall I help you put it on?"

Samson got up and walked behind Sophie to do up the necklace clasp. A delicious shiver travelled the length of her spine as his fingers grazed her neck.

"Happy birthday," he said, and bending down, kissed her on the cheek. Did he linger longer than strictly necessary, or was her imagination running overtime? She fiddled around, putting the card and box into the tray at the bottom of the pushchair to give her face a chance to return to its normal colour and her heart to slow down to its usual rhythm.

* * *

They sat over their meal for a couple of hours, beginning with the delicious antipasti platter of herby focaccia, salami, olives, sundried tomatoes, and grilled peppers and artichoke. Tortelloni stuffed with goat's cheese and smothered in butter, pine nuts, and rosemary with a liberal sprinkling of Parmigiano followed for Sophie and roasted pork belly with fennel and gnocchi for Samson.

When Alana began to get bored, Francesco's wife, Daniela, took the baby for a walk in the pushchair and returned her fast asleep.

Sophie's vanilla panna cotta was the perfect pudding, and, as Alana was still snoring quietly, they even risked an espresso before they wandered slowly back home.

"I've had a wonderful evening," Sophie said closing the front door behind them.

"Good, so have I," said Samson.

Sophie turned and found him rather closer than expected. His eyes met hers and her heart began beating fast. Was he going to kiss her? Samson opened his mouth to speak but was interrupted by Alana letting out a cry from the pushchair as she woke suddenly. The moment was broken.

* * *

Samson smiled softly as he put a tablet in the dishwasher and started a cycle.

Sophie was upstairs with Alana, giving the baby a bottle to help her back to sleep. He could make out some of the murmurings down the monitor, despite trying not to listen. To respect Sophie's privacy, he was doing his absolute best to ignore the monitor's screen, but it warmed his heart to hear the soothing words and Alana's responsive coos.

He considered taking out a bottle of wine, or maybe bringing out the good whisky he had tucked away, but instead filled the kettle and chose two mugs from the cupboard, taking pleasure in his knowledge that he knew Sophie's favourite, and popped a tea bag in each.

It was such a short space of time since the night Natasha had knocked on his door with Alana in her arms, but how his life had changed. When he'd last shared a home with anybody, he'd been at university. He'd landed on his feet straight after his degree and secured a job with a large architectural firm, and had been able to afford his first place by himself — even if it was only a studio flat. He'd never lived with a girlfriend — several years spent working hard so he could set himself up as a very successful freelancer didn't leave much time for serious relationships.

Now here he was, washing up baby bottles while he waited for Sophie to join him, happier and more content than he'd ever been. How bizarre fate could be. When he'd first met Sophie, of course he'd registered how pretty she was with her delicate features and pale green eyes, so full of grief. He'd felt a bolt of attraction, but she'd been so prickly and uptight, so not his type — and not seeming exactly keen for he and Alana to have a relationship — that his focus had been on making sure he got access to his daughter. Inviting Sophie to move in with him had been a means to this, but Samson couldn't deny his feelings about her were now very different, and he was finding it harder and harder to ignore how much he liked her.

He absentmindedly glanced over at the monitor screen again. Sophie was settling Alana into her cot and would be down soon.

He'd been so close to kissing her in the hallway. He hadn't planned to, not that the thought hadn't crossed his mind before, but it had seemed the perfect moment after such a fun evening and his resistance had failed.

It had been for the best when Alana interrupted them though. He wanted to do all he could for Alana and Sophie, he owed them that, and anything romantic happening between himself and Sophie would definitely complicate matters and wouldn't be right in the circumstances. It was great they'd become friends and were getting on so well, but that was how things needed to stay. He hoped he was capable of being as strong as his convictions.

By the time Sophie appeared at the kitchen door, the sweetest smile playing on her lips, Samson had stiffened his resolve.

"Hi," he said cheerfully. "Did she settle?"

"Yeah, the bottle sent her right off. Would you like another drink?" Sophie asked shyly.

"Actually . . . it's getting late and I'm beat. I'm going to head off to bed. There's a cup of tea on the side for you," said Samson with an exaggerated yawn. "I'll see you both in the morning."

"Oh, OK." Disappointment flashed across Sophie's face. "Thank you for the lovely meal, and my beautiful card and present." She fiddled with the necklace as she spoke. "Sleep well."

"You too. It was my pleasure." Samson moved past her and was heading up the stairs before he was tempted to change his mind. He couldn't allow himself to give in and show Sophie exactly how he felt about her.

* * *

A week later, Sophie was on her way back from a meeting in London. She'd been up in the night with a poorly Alana, who was full of cold. She was tired and glad to be almost finished for the day. She was late coming home but would be able to give Alana her bath at least.

Her mobile, attached to the dashboard, flashed with a call from Samson so she pulled over and stopped the car.

"Hi," Sophie said. "Sorry I'm running so late, the meeting overran. I'm almost home. Do you want me to pick up something for supper?"

"Alana's breathing wasn't right," Samson said, hurriedly. "Her chest sounded all rattly and she was a strange colour, so I drove her to the GP. They're calling an ambulance and taking her to the hospital."

Hearing Sophie's sharp intake of breath, he quickly added, "It's just as a precaution, so they can monitor her. They're not one hundred per cent happy with her oxygen levels."

"I'll meet you at the hospital. Are they taking her to the Royal Sussex?"

"Yes. They say they'll take her straight up to the Children's Ward."

"I'll be there as soon as I can." Sophie ended the call.

She took a few deep breaths to calm herself down before starting the car again. Fear flooded through her: the last time she'd been in that hospital, her sister had died. She couldn't lose Alana as well. She knew she was overreacting but wasn't able to stop. Her niece was still so little, and the doctors must have been very concerned about her breathing to have called an ambulance. Sophie berated herself. How could she not have noticed how unwell Alana was? Had she been too busy getting ready for work she'd missed one of the warning signs? She'd read up on so much medical advice since Alana came into her life, she should have seen anything coming! Would Samson blame her? It must be horrible for him dealing with it by himself.

She parked at the hospital, with more upsetting memories of the awful night Natasha had passed away flashing through her mind, and, following the signs as best as she could considering the state she was in, she ran to the Children's Ward.

The reception was unmanned, and Sophie glanced around frantically for help. A nurse approached, and Sophie managed to get her attention.

"Excuse me, I'm looking for Alana Perring? Could you tell me where she is?"

"Are you family?" the nurse asked.

"Yes."

"We're not busy today so we were able to pop her in a side room," explained the nurse. "Number 7, at the end of the corridor to your left. If you head down there, I'll be right behind you. I'm due to check on her."

Sophie thanked the nurse, her fear subsiding thanks to the nurse's calm demeanour; the medical staff were obviously not panicking — but she wouldn't be happy until she'd seen Alana for herself.

She went along the corridor. The door to Alana's room was open, and Samson sat in the armchair next to a cot. He looked up and spotted her at the same time as she saw him.

Alana was wrapped in her father's arms — he held an oxygen mask in front of her face.

Relief at being with her niece fought with her terror at the idea of the baby not being able to breathe without assistance.

"Don't panic," Samson said kindly. "It's a precaution. Hopefully it won't be for long — she's not happy keeping it on." Alana was sleepy and looked very sorry for herself, her blonde hair damp with sweat.

There was a knock at the open door as the nurse who'd directed Sophie came in.

"Hello there," she said to Alana. "I need to take her temperature again," she explained, and produced a thermometer which she held in the little girl's armpit. Alana squirmed a little but didn't complain.

"So, Alana has a bad case of croup," the nurse said to Sophie. "She's had prednisolone and will be fine. She should begin to feel and sound a lot better within the next couple of hours, but we'll need to observe her overnight. We can set up a camp bed by Alana's cot if Mum or Dad would like to stay?" she suggested.

"I'm Alana's aunt . . ." Sophie began. "I'll stay."

"We'll both stay if that's possible," said Samson.

"You're both welcome to, but I'm afraid there's only one pull-out single," the nurse explained, showing them the foldaway bed.

"We'll sort something out," Samson said pleasantly.

The nurse left them, and Sophie took a turn with Alana and her mask so Samson could go to the loo. He returned with coffees.

"I'm glad we're both staying," Sophie said, accepting a cup. "It would be scary to be here all night alone with Alana sounding so awful."

"It would."

"I'm so sorry I didn't realise how ill Alana was," Sophie began, tears pricking at her eyes. "I can't believe I went off to London with her in this state."

"Don't be silly." Samson said immediately, bending down and putting his arm around Sophie and Alana. "She didn't sound anything like this when you left — she had a bit of a cold. There was no way you could have known she'd end up here."

"Thanks for being so nice."

"I'm always nice." He smiled. "I'm fine with Alana for a bit if you want to grab us some food? These drinks are from the kitchen down the hall, but there's a Starbucks on the ground floor which is open for a while yet I think. The sandwiches there are bound to be better than from the cafeteria or a vending machine."

"That's a good plan. I'll go now. I'll be as quick as I can. Have we got everything we'll need for Alana?"

"I reckon so. She's got spare clothes in the changing bag. The nurses have given me some extra nappies, and they have formula and food."

"Should I pop home and pick up some stuff for us?"

"We'll be all right, won't we?" Samson said, seeming worried.

"I guess . . ." Sophie thought she'd appreciate having her toothbrush with her.

"Sorry." Samson seemed more stressed than Sophie had ever seen him before. "It's just, I know I'm being a bit rubbish, but I'd rather you didn't leave us for too long."

Despite everything, Sophie felt her insides lift. This was such a horrible situation, but it was good they felt they were in it together, and touching to hear Samson needed her there with him.

"You're right," she said. "We'll be fine until tomorrow. If it looks like Alana's going to have to stay here for longer, one of us can pop home and grab anything we need."

"I'll organise for someone to take care of Mutt," Samson said. He made a very hurried phone call to a friend who was going to pick him up and have him for the night. Sophie found herself worrying Mutt would miss them and be upset, and wonder why he'd been sent to a strange house — he was such a sensitive soul. She couldn't help liking that daft creature.

* * *

By the time Sophie returned from her supply run with cold drinks, sandwiches and crisps, Alana had been checked again by the doctor, who was so pleased with her progress, she was allowed to go without the oxygen mask. She was gnawing on a piece of toast one of the nurses had made for her as she'd been feeling too bad to eat the tea she'd been offered earlier. Samson had found a second chair, albeit a hard, uncomfortable plastic one, so they could both sit down.

There wasn't any point in trying to keep Alana to her routine that evening as everything else was so different for her, but they attempted to anyway, to give themselves something to do if nothing else.

Alana wasn't keen to go to sleep, despite the fact it was an hour later than they usually put her to bed. She stared at them from her cot as they ate their sandwiches, the adults trying to keep as quiet, and appear as uninteresting, as possible. They even turned the overhead lights off, leaving only the smallest side lamp on.

Finally, Alana gave in and went to sleep. It was only nine, so too early to go to bed themselves. Samson went to get more tea, and came back, looking very proud of himself with a small pile of books he'd found in the parents' lounge.

"Can I interest you in a Dan Brown? Or possibly a Lee Child?"

Sophie screwed up her face.

"Maeve Binchy then? That's my final offer."

"Maeve," Sophie decided. "My mum used to love her books."

"When did she pass away?" Samson asked gently.

"Three years ago last January, about four months after my dad. They both had cancer — Mum in her breast and Dad in his throat."

"That must have been dreadful."

"It was," Sophie admitted. "They both tried to hide it from me for as long as they could — Natasha was travelling, and I think they thought it was too much for me to deal with on my own. I moved back home with them when I found out. It was a really sad time, but I'm glad I had it with them."

"What about Natasha? Did she come home?"

Sophie paused for a second before continuing onto a subject still a little raw, "No. We couldn't get in touch with her. We didn't have a contact number or an address. The only time we'd hear from her was when we received the occasional postcard. When she finally called, it was the week after Mum's funeral. I don't think she saw much point in coming back then, so she didn't. I saw her briefly when she met me at the solicitor's office to finalise Mum and Dad's will settlement."

Sophie became aware tears were running down her cheeks.

"I had no idea . . ." Samson said.

"Why would you?"

Sophie wiped her eyes.

"Would you mind if we changed the subject?" she asked, suddenly realising she was giving away more of her relationship with her sister than she ought to. If she'd said any more, she might have admitted the meeting at the solicitors was the last time she'd seen Natasha, and Samson would realise she hadn't known Alana any longer than he had.

"Of course, no problem," said Samson, giving her a kind smile, which immediately made Sophie feel guilty, however essential she knew her duplicity to be.

They got as comfortable as they could in their chairs, close to one another through necessity so they could see to read by the tiny lamp.

Alana was definitely feeling a bit better, but her breathing was still a little laboured and they both jumped every time she coughed, and would look up to check on her. She wriggled around a lot and didn't seem to go into a proper deep sleep until eleven.

"Shall we turn in?" asked Samson, with a yawn.

"Sure," Sophie answered, feeling suddenly self-conscious.

"You take the bed," he offered. Seeing the uncertainty on Sophie's face, he added, "Honestly, I can sleep anywhere, I'll be fine in the armchair."

They took turns to go down the corridor and use the utilitarian bathroom set aside for parents staying and then settled down as best as they could for the night. Sophie was grateful there was the cot between them, which made it feel less like they were actually sleeping next to each other. Of course all the noises from the rest of the ward and the fact that nurses were coming in regularly to check on Alana, also put an end to any atmosphere of romance which may potentially have been gently hanging in the air.

"Well, goodnight," said Sophie, nonchalantly, turning off the lamp.

"Night," Samson replied.

Sophie naturally thought she should turn away from Samson, so it wasn't like she was watching him, and he wouldn't spot if she slept with her mouth open, but then she wouldn't be able to see Alana and would need to turn over every time she wanted to check on the little girl.

She lay awake for a long time, trying to keep as quiet as possible, both so she didn't disturb Samson, and so she could hear Alana's breathing. The room was not as dark as Sophie was used to sleeping in thanks to a window next to the door letting in light from the corridor outside, despite their closing its blinds. She could make out Samson's outline. The nurse had brought him a blanket which he'd wrapped himself in. A few times when she'd glanced over, he'd been staring out across the room, seemingly deep in contemplation. Once, their eyes had met over the cot. Sophie smiled, but she wasn't sure if it was light enough for him to make that out. He didn't return her smile anyway, and turned away.

Alana was sounding almost completely better by morning and managed plenty of breakfast. The hours seemed to crawl by as they waited for the doctor to come round to confirm they could go home, and then having to hang around for the antibiotics Alana would need to take for the next few days. It was after lunch by the time a very grumpy, sleep-deprived Alana was discharged.

Thankfully, it didn't take long for Sophie to drive them all home.

"It's time for Alana's bottle and then shall I put her down for her nap?" Samson asked as he closed the front door behind them and stifled a yawn himself.

"I'll make up her bottle," Sophie offered. "I don't know about putting her in her room by herself . . . she's exhausted, but I want to keep an eye on her for the rest of the day at least."

"How about I set up the travel cot in the den?"

"Perfect, I'll get us a cup of tea and then I can sit in there with her and veg-out in front of the television while she sleeps."

"Mind if I join you?" asked Samson.

"Of course not. What do you want to watch?"

"Something funny. Have a browse on Netflix?"

Sophie made tea and prepared Alana's bottle before beginning searching the streaming service while Samson put up the travel cot and changed Alana's nappy. He joined her on the sofa and gave Alana her bottle while Sophie continued scrolling. It was hard choosing something they'd both enjoy; she didn't know what he liked to watch. It wasn't something they'd ever discussed.

"How about *Friends*?" Samson suggested, spotting the programme on the suggestions list.

"Really?" asked Sophie incredulously.

"Yeah." He sounded embarrassed. "I like *Friends*, don't you?"

"Sure, I just didn't think you would."

"Let's binge: season one, episode one."

"OK." Sophie laughed.

Alana fell asleep in Samson's arms while she had her bottle. Once he was sure she was absolutely fast asleep, he gently transferred her into the cot, before sitting back down on the sofa with a sigh and downing the last of his tea.

Sophie tried to surreptitiously edge away as much as she possibly could from Samson; being close to him was far too discombobulating with her body telling her it wanted to edge nearer, but her mind firmly reminding her of their very complicated situation. Soon though she became absorbed in the show, settling down into the comfortable sofa and giving in to the exhaustion. Alana's breathing was sounding normal, and so Sophie felt she could relax a little. She felt safe and so happy to be back where she now thought of as home, and her eyes slowly closed.

* * *

The next thing Sophie knew, Alana was gurgling away. Sophie opened her eyes — her niece was sitting up in the travel cot. Then Sophie realised she was leaning against Samson. She'd somehow moved against him while she'd been napping. She got up as swiftly as she could, wiping her mouth as she did to check she hadn't dribbled in her sleep. Oh dear Lord! What would he think of her? She was picking up Alana as Samson began to wake. He stretched languidly and opened his eyes.

"Wow, how long was I asleep?" he asked.

Sophie checked her watch. "About an hour and a half."

"That feels so much better," Samson declared. "How's Alana doing?"

Sophie felt her niece's forehead. "She's not hot, and she's definitely less congested."

"It's a gorgeous afternoon. Do you think she'd like to go down to the beach for a while?"

"That might be a bit much," said Sophie, uncertainly.

"Yeah, maybe you're right."

"You go out though if you want . . ."

"Nah, I'll stay with you two. What if we carried a few bits into the garden for her? She can sit in the shade, and if we're worried about her not feeling well, she can come straight back inside."

"Great," Sophie said. "But are you sure you don't need to go and get some work done?"

"It can wait until tomorrow. What about you?"

"It can wait until tomorrow," Sophie agreed, contentedly.

They each had a quick shower, which made them feel a million times more awake and with it, then put a big rug in the garden for Alana and brought out plenty of her toys. It was amazing how much better the little girl was, though both Sophie and Samson kept a very careful eye on her, and enjoyed the extra cuddles she was wanting to give them. She seemed so happy to be home and not be feeling awful.

Samson went to pick up Mutt once he and Sophie were confident Alana was unlikely to have a relapse.

The dog was also thrilled to be home, and Sophie automatically scooped up her niece as Mutt came racing through the house to find them. But she needn't have worried. Mutt stopped short when he saw Alana, perhaps sensing she hadn't been well, and gave her foot a gentle lick. Alana giggled, pulling away from her aunt to get to her friend, so Sophie put her back down on the rug. Mutt lay down next to Alana. She gave his ear a little tug and went back to playing next to him. They truly were the best of mates.

* * *

Samson took Mutt for a walk while Sophie was bathing Alana and then he went on to the supermarket as the kitchen cupboards were definitely a little bare. Sophie was put under strict instructions that he was going to cook for her. It would only be something simple he said, but he'd sort it.

Alana had her bottle and her story and was put to bed. Delicious smells emanated from the kitchen as Sophie came downstairs. A glass of white wine was poured ready for her on the kitchen table.

"Hey, how's she doing?" Samson asked.

"Really well. Definitely ready for bed though."

Samson caught her debating the wine. "You can have a glass of wine," he said, gently. "She'll be fine tonight, she's doing brilliantly. You can relax."

"You're right," Sophie said, taking a sip. "What's for supper? It smells delicious."

"It's kind of a prawn and watercress pilaf-y thing . . . I'm making it up as I go along."

"That sounds interesting." She laughed. "I'm starving."

"Have some faith! It'll be good. And I've got some garlic flatbread in the oven to keep you going. It'll be ready in five."

"Brilliant. Is there anything I can do?"

"Nope, sit down and entertain me."

Sophie sank down into a kitchen chair. Mutt came over to say hello and she absentmindedly stroked his head. A heavy, grey paw tapped her insistently until she gave him her full attention for a minute, then, when he was satisfied, he slumped down at her feet. She glanced over at the baby monitor: Alana seemed to be fine.

The flatbread went down well, taking the edge off Sophie's hunger, and she poured herself another half glass of wine after giving in and checking on Alana upstairs. She was of course fast asleep and breathing normally.

Samson hummed while he cooked. It didn't take Sophie long to realise it was the *Friends* theme song he had stuck in his head. She added in the claps at the opportune moment. "What is it with you and that show? It wouldn't be my first choice if I had to guess a TV programme you'd enjoy," she said, laughing.

"Maria and Bethan used to love it so it was always on in our house," he answered. "And it's funny! Who doesn't like *Friends*?"

"Monsters! Everyone should like *Friends*," she said.

Samson spotted her glancing over at the baby monitor again. "She's fine, don't worry. The hospital did an amazing job and she's so much better now. Hopefully, she'll sleep brilliantly tonight and will be back to her smiley self tomorrow."

"You're right, she's bounced back amazingly quickly." She shook her head. "It was so scary to see her with the oxygen mask." Tears threatened to fall at the memory of the previous day.

"I know, but it doesn't help to dwell on it. I'm just so thankful we're back home and she didn't need to stay in for any longer."

"I think another night would have broken me!"

"It wasn't a night I'm keen to repeat any time soon," Samson agreed.

* * *

The pair ate their delicious meal, reminiscing over their favourite *Friends* episodes, and generally making the most of being home again.

The couple of glasses of wine she'd drunk meant Sophie was feeling far more candid than usual. She debated with herself; the atmosphere was so relaxed, so natural she didn't want to do anything to spoil it, but there were some things she needed to know, had wanted to know for a long time. The alcohol made her brave: "So . . . tell me about you and my sister . . ."

"What about us?" asked Samson, cagily.

"How did you meet?"

"At a party," he said. "Natasha knew a couple of my friends. She'd been travelling with them years ago, and had only recently moved to Brighton."

"How long did you date for?"

"It couldn't truly be classed as proper dating," answered Samson, looking like he'd rather not be having this conversation. "We hung out together for a few weeks. I tried to teach her to surf," he said, with a little smile at the memory. "Then we kind of drifted apart. The next time I saw her was almost a year and a half later when she turned up on my doorstep. The night she died."

"Did you love her?" Sophie wasn't able to stop herself from asking the question she was so, so desperate to know the answer to.

"No," he answered after a pause. "I sort of wish I had. We had a child together and now she's gone, and I barely knew her, and that makes me feel sadder than the fact she's gone . . . if that even makes any sense."

"I get it," said Sophie. "I feel kind of the same way about Natasha. She was always a worry to our parents and made home life very difficult. She was the archetypal awful teenager, but rather than growing out of that, it seemed to get worse. It culminated when she stole a lot of money from them and disappeared. I told you when our parents died, Natasha was travelling and I couldn't get hold of her. She was funding her travels with their money. She tried to get in touch again months later when she returned to the UK, said she was living in Brighton, but I told her I wanted nothing to do with her, and I hadn't seen her since."

"You didn't know what was going to happen," Samson said kindly. "You were hurt by her actions."

He was being so understanding, and so supportive, Sophie didn't feel she could hide the truth from him anymore, and she said slowly, "That meant I didn't know she got pregnant. I didn't know anything about Alana until after Natasha died."

Samson was silent as he contemplated what she'd said. He took a sip of wine, then asked, "Why didn't you tell me before? I assumed you'd known Alana her whole life, had been part of her upbringing from day one."

"I know, and I let you believe that because I was scared you'd use it against me. I thought you'd try to take Alana away from me if you were aware I was a stranger to her until the night she was handed to me by a friend of Natasha's."

Samson was silent, taking in everything she said before replying, "Perhaps you were right. You have done the most fantastic job looking after Alana, and there's no way I would even contemplate you not having the role in her life you do now, but if I'd known straight away that you'd only just met her too, I think I may have tried to insist you handed her over to me."

"I really am sorry for keeping it a secret for so long. I should have trusted you with the truth before now."

"I understand," he said. "It's good it's out in the open now. As we're being this . . . direct, I had something I wanted to broach with you . . ."

"OK . . ." Sophie said, uncertainly.

"At the hospital, they called Alana, Alana Perring . . . which I know is her name, but . . . I'd like her to have my surname. She's my daughter after all . . ."

"You want her to drop her mother's surname?" Sophie said incredulously. Her surname was one of the few things Alana would have of her mother's, a bond between them. Samson couldn't take that.

"No, no!" said Samson quickly, immediately realising the sudden change in atmosphere and Sophie's mood. "I was hoping to add my surname — I was thinking Perring-Smith. I would never take her mother's surname from her! You don't need to give me a response right away, but it's important to me that you're happy with it."

"I . . . am," said Sophie, calming down quickly and again breathing easily. "I think it's a lovely idea — and thank you for asking my opinion. That means a lot."

Samson smiled back at her. "Not a problem. I'm so glad you're OK with it. It means a lot to me." He nodded his head towards the garden. "Shall we take the rest of this wine outside? It's a gorgeous evening."

"Yeah, let me grab a jumper."

"Meet you out there," Samson said, easily. "No checking on Alana when you go upstairs — she's fine, and you'll wake her up."

"I'm making no promises." Sophie cast an eye over the monitor as she got up to leave the room; her niece was still asleep.

"I tell you what." Samson caught her gently by the arm before she went through the door. "Put this on. It'll save you the trip upstairs, and prevent you from being tempted to prod Alana awake to check she's all right."

He grabbed a hooded sweatshirt of his which had been draped over the back of a kitchen chair.

Before she could protest, he said, "Arms up." She obeyed instinctively, lifting her arms high as he slipped the top over her head and pulled it down into place. The intense smell of him was almost more than Sophie could bear, making her feel giddy as it surrounded her, and she did her very best to act normally.

"There we go," he said. "All toasty now."

Their eyes met. Sophie felt she should turn away, but she found she didn't want to.

His hands were still on the bottom of the hoodie from when he'd been pulling it into place.

They were both locked in position, gazing at each other. Samson reached his arm up and gently lifted Sophie's hair out from where it was caught inside the hoodie, tucking it behind her ears. His eyes never left hers.

Sophie's whole body was tense and alert, anticipating what was going to happen, as Samson's hand slowly moved round so he was cupping the back of her neck. He stopped and raised an eyebrow questioningly. Sophie responded by tilting up her head ready to meet his lips and suddenly they were kissing, and nothing else mattered.

CHAPTER 11

Sophie woke up in Samson's bed the next morning. The clock in the corner told her it was quarter past seven; Alana would be awake soon.

Remembering the night before brought a smile to her face. Samson had lived up to her every fantasy. Leading her upstairs to his room, he'd made love to her, making her feel like the most beautiful woman in the world. The chemistry and attraction she'd been feeling hadn't been wrong — they were so very good together.

Afterwards, he had got up, and she wondered if he wanted her to leave and sleep in her own bedroom, but he'd said, "I'm going to get some water and let Mutt out. I'll be back in five."

Sophie had used the opportunity to take a quick peep at Alana and was pleased her breathing sounded absolutely fine. Then she'd climbed back into Samson's bed, eager for him to return. He hadn't been long and had spooned around her, whispering, 'Good night' into her neck. She still couldn't believe it had happened.

Now Samson was fast asleep on the other side of the bed. Sophie watched his chest gently moving up and down, and resisted the urge to stroke his beautiful hair off his face, not wanting to disturb him. She decided to get up so she could at least wash and put some make-up on before facing him. Sophie slipped out of the bed and padded along the hallway to the bathroom and showered. Then she went into her bedroom, blow-dried her hair and fussed around deciding what to wear before getting dressed.

She was finishing when she heard Samson go into Alana's room. She went to join him, nervous butterflies bouncing about inside her.

Samson was talking to Alana and changing her nappy. "Good morning, you two," Sophie said.

"Morning," Samson replied, not meeting her eyes. "Could you get Alana's bottle on? We'll be down in a minute."

"Sure." Sophie was hurt and disappointed by Samson's demeanour, but hoped she was being oversensitive. Perhaps he was concentrating on changing Alana or was anxious himself about what her feelings would be regarding the previous night.

She prepared Alana's bottle and began to make coffee. Samson and Alana came into the kitchen. Alana reached out for her aunt and Samson passed the baby over to her, still managing not to look directly at her.

"Coffee's nearly ready," Sophie said, overly cheerfully.

"Thanks, but I think I'll hop in the shower first. Are you OK to give Alana her milk?"

"Yeah, enjoy your shower!" Sophie said as breezily as she could.

Alone with her niece, Sophie pondered what to do — was she worrying too much? Maybe Samson had a bit of a headache from the wine the night before? His being a little offhand with her didn't *have* to mean he regretted what had happened between them. He'd probably be back to normal with her when he came back downstairs.

But Samson didn't return. She heard the shower going and then stop, and a few minutes later the bathroom door opened. Sophie finished giving Alana a bottle and then made some porridge, which she fed her while she ate her own breakfast.

Eventually, Sophie gave up waiting for him. She reheated his coffee in the microwave while she cleaned Alana up, and decided to take his drink to him.

She checked Samson's bedroom first, but the door was open and he wasn't in there, so he must be in the study, the door of which was firmly shut.

Sophie knocked as best as she could while carrying a wiggly Alana and a full mug of hot liquid. "Come in," came the response after a pause.

She pushed open the door. Samson was working on his laptop and didn't glance up as she came in.

"I brought you your coffee," she said, putting it down next to him.

"Thank you." He finally met her gaze, obviously realising he was being really rude. "I've got a bit caught up here. Do you mind having Alana for a while?"

"No, that's fine." She was going to leave but stopped herself. "Samson," she said firmly. "What's going on?"

"What do you mean?"

"You know what I mean."

Samson sighed, and put his head in his hands. "I'm sorry . . . I didn't know how to deal with the situation, with what happened last night . . . and now I've been acting like a complete bastard haven't I?"

"Pretty much." Sophie was honest. She was feeling very vulnerable. She held Alana closer still.

Samson got up and came over to them. "Last night was wonderful, but I think it happened because we were both so relieved Alana was home from the hospital and was so much better," he began, "and the wine certainly added to me doing something which, if I'd been thinking properly, I would have realised was not a very good idea." He paused, evidently checking Sophie's face for her reaction. She focused on appearing impassive and expressionless, the only thing she could think of to stop herself from crying.

"I'm still struggling to work out how to be a dad, and we're looking after Alana together here . . . There have been

so many changes, for both of us, so quickly . . . it's too cha-
otic. It wouldn't be sensible for us to start up a romantic
relationship at the moment. What if it went horribly wrong?
Alana . . . Natasha . . . It's too . . . complicated."

"Well, thanks for letting me know," Sophie managed
to say.

"Hey," Samson said, taking her and Alana in his arms.
"I think you're amazing, you know that and I'm so sorry to
hurt you, but I'm not ready for a relationship, and it's going
to be so much harder breaking up a few months down the
line. I think this is for the best."

Sophie pulled away; him holding her was making things
a million times worse.

"You're probably right," she said, doing all she could to
harden herself. "We need to focus on Alana. She's already
had far too much upheaval. She's got to be our priority."

"You're sure you're OK?"

"I'm fine." She turned to leave.

"Are you going to take Alana out?" Samson asked, obviously trying to restore some normality to their conversation.

Sophie paused in the doorway. "No, I know she's loads
better, but I think we ought to keep her at home for a bit, at
least until she's off the antibiotics. I'll let Julia know we won't
be going to baby group this afternoon."

Sophie so wished she could take Alana out somewhere,
anywhere, so she could get some space from Samson until she
was able to get herself in check, but the poor baby had only
been in the hospital the day before, and it would be dreadful
if she had a relapse.

"That sounds sensible."

"I'll see you later then." Sophie moved swiftly into the
hall before her tears started to fall.

She carried Alana into her bedroom and placed her on
the floor with a load of her toys. Then, closing the door, she
allowed herself to give in and cry.

It felt like she'd been so close to having everything she'd
ever wanted, everything that had been missing from her

previous life when she'd felt so alone and unloved since her parents had passed away. So close to being a proper family with the two people she cared about more than anything else in the world.

She'd managed to control her feelings towards Samson, to keep them at bay to a large extent, because, yes, he was right. Their relationship would not be straightforward, both because of them needing to work together for Alana, but also due to his past history with Natasha. But the night before had felt like she'd opened the floodgates of her attraction to him. She was in no doubt that she had feelings for him, strong feelings, and his actions had led her to believe he felt at least something of the same. To have his affection whisked away from her, well, it was even worse than not experiencing it at all. And now they'd messed things up with their friendship too. How could they go back to how easy they'd become together? They'd always have this hanging over them.

The fear Samson would come checking to ensure she wasn't upset was enough to force Sophie to pull herself back from fully giving in to her emotions. Now, that would be excruciatingly embarrassing. She'd just have to pretend last night hadn't happened, for Alana's sake, because if she and Samson couldn't work together it was back to her old fears of a custody battle. And he had a much better claim on Alana than she did. Especially now he knew she'd only met her niece a matter of weeks ago. If he chose to use that against her, she wasn't sure what part she'd be able to play in her niece's life, and the thought terrified her.

* * *

Two weeks went by. Two weeks of Sophie and Samson tip-toeing around one another, trying to act as if everything was fair and sunny between them, though it so clearly wasn't.

Sophie was even more grateful for her friend, Julia, who provided a much-needed refuge and counselling service. She relished the times Samson went out surfing or walked Mutt alone, so she had the house to herself and didn't have to play at being all fine and normal.

She kept repeating to herself that things would get better, the hurt she was feeling would lessen, and if this was what she had to endure in order for her to live with her niece, then she was more than willing to bear it. But the thought remained that she'd been so close to having *it*. What she'd always, deep down, wanted. A family. A close, loving, happy family. The feeling of loss wouldn't go away. It followed her around, like a dark cloud, wherever she was and whatever she was doing. What she felt for Samson . . . it was love. All-consuming, heart-rending love. She hadn't seen it through the tumult, but she'd been falling for him since the first time he'd knocked at the door of Natasha's flat. And now, she'd lost him. The sadness, the sensation of loss . . . it took her back to the night of the crash. Unresolved grief, guilt . . . It all entwined into a leaden ball inside her, and as hard as she tried, she could feel it dragging her slowly down.

She couldn't move out, not right away anyway, though what she wanted to do was to get as far away from Samson as possible. To forget anything had ever happened between them. But she had to be with Alana, and attempting to move the little girl out of her father's home would, she feared, bring things to a head regarding custody of Alana rather quickly.

* * *

Sophie was so grateful she had her work to keep her occupied after Alana had gone to bed for the night. Her clients were pleased with her work, and she was getting more through word of mouth. She loved the freedom of working for herself and knowing she could drop everything if she needed to for her niece.

Though it was much more convenient for Sophie to work in the study rather than the kitchen table, she only did so when Samson wasn't also in there: staring at him at the desk opposite was more than she could bear. Even if she managed not to look in his direction at all, she was sure she could feel his eyes on her as he tiptoed around her, the guilt that he knew he'd hurt her so evident on his face.

She had some client documents to print out and then be posted that afternoon, so was glad when Samson said he was going to take Alana and Mutt out for an hour; she could use the printer in the office in peace. She printed what she needed, and addressed the envelope, but realised she didn't have a stapler — goodness only knew where hers had vanished to during the super speedy packing up of her flat.

She walked round to Samson's desk to see if he had one she could borrow. The top of his desk was quite messy, but there was no stapler hiding in amongst the piles of papers. Absentmindedly she pulled open the top drawer on the side of the desk, thinking that would be where she'd keep a stapler; he'd told her more than once she was welcome to use any of his office supplies, and it wasn't locked.

The drawer was a catch-all, packed full of random pens, elastic bands, receipts, and goodness only knew what else, making it difficult to get at what was inside. Her heart stopped as she saw what was written on a piece of paper stuffed in the top — they were the results of a paternity test. She pulled the paper out, careless in her hurry, scanning it swiftly to discover the results: it confirmed Samson was Alana's father. Sophie subconsciously let out a sigh of relief, Samson and Alana loved each other so much, and had such a close bond, it would be devastating for Samson if he'd discovered he wasn't really Alana's father.

But her feeling of joy evaporated even swifter than it had come: he'd had the test done without her knowledge. The letter was only dated three days before. He'd had Alana tested and not said a word to her.

Why would he do that?

Because he'd decided to pursue sole custody and wanted DNA evidence to support his claim?

She couldn't help but wonder what else he might be hiding. Checking underneath, she found her undeniable proof of his intentions: court papers. Adoption papers. Presumably what he needed because of not being registered on Alana's birth certificate.

Sophie dropped the bundle as if it had burnt her, her instinct to bury it where she'd uncovered it as if doing so could turn back her ever having found it. Or better still, make Samson, of all people, not be deceiving her in this way. It couldn't be anything else. There couldn't be another explanation.

They hadn't properly talked about what they were going to do formally with Alana, other than that they would work together to bring her up, but what had happened between the two of them to have changed his mind? He'd obviously regretted sleeping with her, but would that have spurred him to this? And she'd told him she'd only found out about Alana the night Natasha died of course! It was the perfect ammunition against her. That one fact weakened her whole guardianship case, and he wanted to use it against her. Oh, why had she ever thought it would be safe to confide in him? She was an idiot. How could she not have known any man her sister had had anything to do with would turn out to be completely untrustworthy?

He was doing his level best to get her out of the picture for good. He was trying to take their little girl. For him to have the best chance of success, she guessed it made sense for him to prepare everything in secret, build his case ready, then spring it all upon her. And expect her to fold without a fight?

Crushed by his betrayal, she broke down, her soul devastated.

CHAPTER 12

Rooted to the spot in the study, Sophie wavered, unable to move, unsure what to do. She never should have let her guard down with Samson. But how could she not have? She'd been blinded by her wishful thinking into a misleading dream, a dream that he wanted the same as she did and had the same feelings about her as she did for him. And that they could become a real parental unit for Alana.

It was easy to see why he was preparing and had kept his cards so close to his chest. He adored Alana and seemed to have settled into fatherhood naturally and easily. Why would he want her aunt hanging around? He didn't need Sophie, he could easily afford a babysitter or a nanny. He had no loyalty to her, they had no history, other than that he'd slept with her and her sister — both relationships over as soon as they started — though, granted, it sounded like her sister had lasted slightly longer than she had. Having her stay may have been handy at the beginning when he had no idea what to do with Alana, but now her usefulness to him had expired.

Maybe. But in reality, she knew the truth: she'd given him the ammunition to use against her. That night, their night, she'd confessed how precarious her link to Alana was, that Natasha had hidden Alana from her too and her discovery of the baby wasn't until after the terrible crash. That Alana hadn't known her aunt.

Was there anything she could do? Anything that would mean she'd stand a chance if it came to a fight in court over Alana? She had nothing concrete in writing from Natasha to say she'd want Sophie to care for her baby. Having checked through all of her sister's worldly goods, Sophie knew her sister hadn't left a will. But Natasha had chosen not to tell Samson about their child for months, she must have had a reason. He'd more than shown his worth as a father in the time since, but could she leverage Natasha's initial reluctance to include him in their daughter's life? And she was Natasha's only relative, Alana's only relative on her mother's side, surely that must give her some rights? But would it just get Sophie an afternoon once a fortnight with Alana?

That wasn't enough. Alana was all Sophie had, was everything to her, was the reason and meaning in her life: she had no partner, no children, no home of her own anymore. She couldn't let her go. There was nothing more important to her than her niece.

Should she leave and take Alana with her? But where would she go? How would she support herself and Alana, moving again? There were so many thoughts fighting through her mind, each desperate to receive the attention it deserved.

She heard the front door open and Samson call out he was back. What should she do?

Her mind raced. Flight or fight, she guessed. But what was best for Alana?

Samson's voice echoed up from the kitchen, searching for her. Damn it! She needed more time. Time to organise her thoughts, sort through her feelings, weigh the options. She had to think about what was truly best for Alana — she needed her father, true, but she also needed a mother. And Sophie was the closest thing to her mother. She couldn't have loved the little girl more if she'd been her own biological daughter.

She hurriedly shoved the papers back where she'd found them and tried to dry her tears carefully with her sleeve, not wanting to smudge her make-up and signal her distress.

Samson's voice had reached the bottom of the stairs. She quickly slipped out of the study.

"I was in the bathroom. Did you enjoy your outing?" she said as nonchalantly as possible, heading him off before he managed to reach the landing.

"Yeah, it was nice. We had ice creams . . ." He trailed off when he saw her face; he could clearly tell she wasn't right. "You OK?" he continued with concern.

"I'm fine," she answered curtly and wanting to end the conversation as quickly as possible.

Obviously not convinced, but warned off by her tone he said, "I've got half Alana's ice cream on my shirt . . . I need to change but I'll be downstairs in a minute . . . if you've got time to talk?"

"Sure," she said, trying to modulate her tone to allay his immediate unease, a plan forming as she thought on her feet. She passed him and walked downstairs. Samson watched her back for a moment before heading to his bedroom.

Alana was in her playpen, 'talking' to Mutt on the other side of the bars. She smiled broadly and gurgled in pleasure as Sophie bent over her. Picking the baby up, her traitorous body gave a tingle of pleasure at Samson's scent surrounding his daughter. She gave Mutt a goodbye pat, grabbed the changing bag and her car keys, and silently left.

* * *

Walking through the downstairs, something immediately struck Samson as wrong. It was . . . he was unsure, then realised: it was too quiet. He saw the playpen he'd put Alana in was empty, and he again searched for Sophie. He went into the garden, but Sophie and Alana weren't out there. Perhaps upstairs? he thought uncertainly. Passing back through the hall, goosebumps rose on his arms as he spotted the changing bag missing. They always put it in the same place: leftmost coat hook. He'd hung it there not five minutes ago. Running to the first floor, calling out their names he checked Alana's room then Sophie's. Nothing. The bathroom door was ajar, and that room empty too. He checked his study: also deserted. But his searching gaze, and knowledge something was very wrong, drew him to his desk. The top drawer wasn't properly closed. Opening it fully, he withdrew the topmost papers. The court documents. The adoption papers he'd got for Sophie, his gift to her, the papers to formally make her the mother she already was. Sticking out from under the first sheet was the positive paternity test.

Oh God. He felt suddenly cold. She'd misunderstood horribly. He could easily construe her reasoning: he was trying to take Alana from her; the test, the forms, the awkwardness of the past weeks — all crystal clear. But . . . so wrong. Crossing to the sash window, he wrenched it up and leaning dangerously out, checked far down the street. Her car had vanished. The love of his life and his daughter had left him.

His faculties momentarily whirled with a cacophony of emotional discord, but within seconds, calm order had been imposed. He could fix this. Logically, she couldn't have got far, and given the fresh tears on the page, the discovery had happened only moments ago, so their flight was unlikely to have been premeditated. He quickly checked Alana's bedroom for confirmation — nothing missing that he could see, no clothes, nappies or other baby supplies seemed to be absent, other than those which would have been in the changing bag. Going into Sophie's room, he swiftly surveyed the space. Thank goodness! The box of Natasha's keepsakes was still here. She wouldn't go for ever without that for Alana he was sure. It was 4.35 p.m. now. Without any expectation of an answer, he tried calling her mobile: nothing.

Where would she have gone? Back to London? He didn't know much about her London life, her haunts, her favourite hideaways. Her old flat was let out, he knew, so not there. Though would she honestly think of her old life first? He hesitated, no — it would be Brighton. He'd check the park, the playground, even Natasha's old flat — though that too was likely to have a new tenant. And he'd call her friend — what was her name? Janet? Julia? Yes, that was it, he had the number in his phone. Though how helpful she'd be and whether he could trust her answers, he didn't know.

* * *

"Damn it!" Samson cursed as he struck the steering wheel of the pick-up with his fist. It was nearly seven. He'd been driving futilely about for almost two and a half hours. Though 'driving' had almost been an exaggeration — peak time, the tourist season, and a beautiful day had all conspired to reduce driving to crawling. He'd eventually covered everywhere he could think of and had even met with an extremely hostile Julia, who'd been as helpful as he'd anticipated. Still, he was pretty certain she had no idea where Sophie and his daughter were. Mutt whined forlornly from where he was spread out over the back seats: he knew something was very wrong. And not just the fact he hadn't been given his tea yet.

Samson had stopped in the hospital car park — he'd been that desperate he'd even checked there — and was marshalling his thoughts for his next move. London? He guessed so. It didn't seem . . . right. As he'd suspected, Natasha's old flat had seemed to be occupied with new tenants, but they weren't in when he called. He'd driven about the area without luck but there was the extremely remote chance they might know something. He decided to swing past there once more in case they were now in, before heading off to London. He was almost there anyway, he had nothing to lose.

The direct road was closed due to road works, so he followed the detour. Taken down towards the beach, he passed the by now fairly empty, seaside car park. What was that? Had it been Sophie's car? He recklessly slammed on his brakes and did a sharp U-turn. The traffic and Mutt all vocally voiced their disapproval, but he was heedless. It was her car. Drawing to a halt with a squeal of brakes next to it, he jumped out of the cab. Her car was empty. But they must be here somewhere. Close. She wouldn't be able to get far across the stones with Alana even if she'd taken the buggy with her. He scanned up and down the beach. The tide was way, way out and the stick figures scattered widely over the large area were all indistinguishable. OK. He could wait here, for them to get back. But he was too worked up with emotion for that. He had to be doing something. He'd take Mutt. They'd walk back and forth in expanding arcs, keeping the car as the focal point — he had to keep an eye on it. He was going to find his family because that's exactly what Alana and, yes, Sophie, were to him now. He had to make this right.

* * *

Sophie gazed out across the sand to the band of blue-grey of the horizon. The sun was low and red and ochre blushed out in the far distance. She could smell the sea from here, where she sat, high up on the beach with Alana fast asleep in her arms.

She hadn't known where to go when she first fled the house. She figured Samson would quickly be after them, but she needed space to think. To decide how to proceed before some heated confrontation. So, she kept moving, aimlessly drifting about, before slowly — inexorably even — being drawn back here. It had a poetic symbolism, she supposed.

This is where it had all started. Her journey. At the end of that horrible night when her sister died, this is the spot where she came, carrying Alana. And at the dawn of the new day, this was where she'd promised to be a mother to this precious little girl. She'd sworn to look after her and be there for her. Always.

That sunrise had been a rebirth for her, her niece a price-less gift that had put colour and meaning into what had been an empty life. She grieved and regretted losing her sister, of course she did, to the very bottom of her soul. But at the same time, she couldn't be without her little girl. And she'd met Samson. She'd cried herself empty over him and his betrayal, but she loved him still. It was silly she knew. They'd had one night together, had been a 'couple' for a matter of hours. She hadn't seen what she had, known fully what she felt until it was over, her seemingly perfect man gone.

She'd criticised him for his underhandedness, but she'd hardly been a paragon of virtue in that regard herself. She'd sought to represent the truth in her own best interest, kept him in the dark about her real relationship with Natasha and Alana, and manoeuvred to cement herself foremost as her niece's guardian, and to keep him out, she realised. She'd wanted him there for Alana — and for her, she confessed — and so valued the love he'd given his daughter — but she'd never given him the respect he'd deserved, never treated him truly equally; always been amazed when Samson had shown himself to be vastly more than she'd initially thought him to be.

So much of this was of her own making she concluded. It didn't change anything: what had happened, had happened. Her chance at blissful happiness was gone. But she was Alana's mother now. The baby needed her, as much as she needed Alana. She wasn't going to hand her over to Samson and disappear quietly. No matter the cost. But she didn't want to separate father and daughter either. That wouldn't be right in any sense. She had to treat him justly; for his sake and Alana's. She'd try to speak to him. Try to form a truce and avoid the irreversible harm a custody battle would exact on them all.

She should move out at once, and offer to divide Alana's time evenly between them. Get his name on her niece's birth certificate and legally seek joint guardianship. To earn his trust, she needed to trust him.

* * *

A shape rapidly lolloping across the beach drew her from her introspection. Mutt. Joy flooded through her, then the wet shaggy form was on her. He licked her enthusiastically in-between excited barks, very proud of himself for finding her. His soggy tail slapped against her in a tornado of affection. She fended him off lovingly, and looking around, sure enough, saw Samson approaching.

"Hey," he said gently.

"Hi," she responded quietly. His chest heaved with the effort of searching for her and the breeze ruffled his hair.

He sat down next to her. "I've been searching for you for hours. I saw you found the papers."

She nodded in affirmation.

"I know what you're feeling and I want to explain. It's not what you think." When Sophie didn't comment, he took it as leave to continue. "I should have told you I was doing the paternity test."

"Yes, you should."

"Yvonne advised me to do it."

"I didn't think you'd go behind my back though."

"I had to be sure and I was too embarrassed to share my fears with you," Samson explained, softly.

"You weren't sure Alana was yours?" asked Sophie, shocked.

"There was still some doubt in my mind."

"But she looks so like you, and you fit so well together."

"I know, but she's a baby — you can convince yourself she looks like anyone. I wasn't in contact with Natasha for a long time, and then she was on my doorstep with a child she said was mine . . ."

"You didn't trust her."

"I know she was your sister and . . ."

"But she wasn't always the most truthful, or reliable of people," Sophie finished for him.

Samson seemed relieved. "I suspected she needed money. I thought that might be why she'd come to see me. Claiming Alana was mine would have been a very convenient way to get a steady income from me."

"I like to think Natasha wouldn't have behaved like that, or at least wouldn't have been able to go through with it. But honestly, I can't be sure. She did steal from Mum and Dad. I know she eventually came to regret doing so, but . . ." She trailed off. She could understand his scepticism. She guessed he'd be an idiot if he wasn't suspicious given the circumstances. Though why not do the test earlier?

"But why did you wait to have it done? Why now?" she continued.

"Because I felt too guilty," Samson said, looking away.

"Guilty?" said Sophie. This wasn't what she expected. "About what? Wanting to take Alana? Or what . . ."

"What?" Samson interrupted immediately. "No, no. I would never take Alana away from you. Never," he said firmly. "You're her mother now. No part of this was about that."

Sophie felt uninvited tears pour down her face with relief at his words. She still didn't understand, couldn't match her interpretation of events with what he was saying, but could she somehow have been wrong? "Then what do you feel guilty about?" she found herself asking.

"I killed Natasha."

"What?" She was stunned for a moment. "Of course you didn't!"

"I'm responsible. It's all my fault," he explained. "She came to see me with Alana, at the house . . . she was upset when I didn't respond the way she wanted. I was thrown, she turned up out of the blue. I didn't believe her, and I told her I didn't. She lost her temper, threw Alana's birth certificate at me and stormed off. Then she got in her car and . . . If I'd reacted better, if she hadn't felt she and Alana had been rejected . . . she wouldn't have been so wound up. And wouldn't have crashed her car and died. It's my fault Alana lost her mother. And you your sister."

Samson was crying now.

"Oh Samson, is this honestly how you've felt?"

"Yes." He nodded. "That's why I broke things off with you. I couldn't be with you, let you trust me, knowing my part in your sister's death. However much I wanted to be with you, I couldn't . . . no matter how great I think we could be together."

Sophie pulled him to her. "Natasha dying was nothing to do with you or anything you did. She was an adult, responsible for her own actions and her own choices. I don't blame you for not believing her. No one would. She was always volatile and impulsive. Her death was a terrible accident. It's a miracle Alana wasn't in the car. Thank God Natasha dropped her off with a friend. That's what we need to focus on."

"Do you mean that? You don't blame me?"

"Of course I don't! You reacted as anyone would. If there's one person who should feel guilty, it's me — Natasha was on her way to deliver a letter to me when she crashed."

"But that doesn't mean her accident . . ."

"Exactly," interrupted Sophie, softly. "Neither of us was to blame for Natasha's death."

"I wish I'd spoken to you about this before."

"So do I."

Sophie took Samson's face in her hands and gently kissed his tears away. He smiled and kissed her back on her mouth. "Do you think you might be willing to give me a second chance? I think I've been a bit of an idiot. The last couple of weeks have been awful. I was trying to do the right thing. I thought I was terrible wanting you. With Natasha's death . . . But everything was so much worse when I let you go. And I realised how much I'd lost and how much I was hurting you."

"I think I'd be willing to give things another try." Sophie smiled as she kissed him again.

Samson pulled away. "I need to explain about the adoption papers."

"It's OK. I understand. Alana means just as much to you as she does to me. You were protecting yourself."

"No! The adoption papers weren't for me. With the paternity test result, I can prove Alana is mine, I don't need to adopt her," Samson explained. "They were for you. I thought . . . well, I thought that no matter what . . . with how things had got between us . . . well, that way you'd always be her mother."

"Really?" Sophie asked, her turn to well up again.

"Really. I want us to bring up Alana together, for us to be a family. It's all I want," said Samson honestly.

"It's all I want too," said Sophie, hardly daring to believe what was happening.

"I love you," Samson said softly.

"I love you too," whispered Sophie and Samson put his arm around her.

They kissed again but were soon interrupted as Alana let out a discontented squawk at being squished between them, and Mutt graced them both with a congratulatory lick, desperate not to be left out of anything.

"I think we'd better get this little one home to bed," said Samson, stroking his daughter's head.

"Absolutely," agreed Sophie.

Samson stood and, taking her hand, pulled her up. "We can never bring back Alana's mother for her, however much we wish we could. But she's got two loving parents who'll do anything in their power to make her happy."

Mutt gave a little bark.

"And she's got a loyal hound to protect her." Sophie gave the dog an affectionate scratch behind the ear.

They stood for a moment gazing out at the sunset before heading back up the beach together, ready to put the past behind them and focus on making the best future for themselves and Alana.

EPILOGUE

It was freezing at the beach, but the rain was doing its best to hold off so at least they were dry, Sophie mused as she watched Samson and Alana by the water's edge. Alana was sitting on her father's shoulders laughing at Mutt running into the sea and being chased back to shore by a wave.

There was still so much to do before Alana's birthday party that Sophie had been reluctant to agree to Samson's idea to go for a walk in the cold, but she was glad they had. Mutt needed a run anyway and the fresh air was very welcome.

The idea of hosting their first children's party was frankly terrifying, even if Sophie had, of course, had it perfectly planned and organised for over a month, much to Samson's amusement.

Samson walked up the beach and waited for Sophie to join him and Alana, who was busy sticking a finger in his left ear.

"This exact spot is where I first told you I loved you," said Samson when Sophie reached him.

"It is indeed," Sophie replied with a grin. Alana was losing a shoe, so Sophie reached up and sorted it out for her. "It's also where I first told you I loved you," she added.

They held hands and looked out at the water. The wind was beginning to pick up and the sea was getting rougher.

A couple of hardy all weather swimmers were aborting their mission a few metres away.

"I can't believe she's one already," said Sophie.

"I know," Samson agreed.

"Do you think Natasha would approve of how she's spending her birthday?"

"I can't imagine Natasha organising a party at the local community centre but I think she'd approve," said Samson, pulling Sophie in for a hug. "Alana's having a great day and Natasha would be happy about that."

"We'd better head home soon," said Sophie, "I need to pick up the cake and finish filling the party bags . . ."

"I can pick up the cake," reassured Samson. "And Alana can come with me so that you can get everything sorted in peace."

"Thank you," said Sophie, gratefully.

"Before we leave though, I had something I wanted to ask you . . . Alana, can you give Mummy this?"

He produced a little black box from Alana's coat pocket and handed it to the baby, who giggled at it, fascinated. Samson bent down so she could hand it to Sophie.

Wordlessly, Sophie accepted it and opened the box. She stared at the beautiful diamond ring inside, tears forming in her eyes.

Looking up, Samson was down on one knee with a wiggly Alana eager to get down.

"I should have anticipated something would go wrong with this," he muttered as he shifted his daughter into his arms. Sophie smiled.

"Sophie Perring. I love you and I want to spend the rest of my life loving you. Will you marry me?" he said. Naturally, Mutt decided it was the perfect time to bound over and attempt to give his master a lick.

"Mutt!" Samson cried. "We're trying to have a moment here!"

Sophie laughed. She took the ring out of the box and relieved him of Alana, who wanted her box back.

"Of course I'll marry you," she said, as Samson got to his feet. "Though I can't believe you entrusted the ring to a one-year-old."

"It seemed like a good idea at the time," Samson explained, with a shrug. He took the ring from her and placed it on her finger. "The main thing is you said yes."

They kissed.

"Was there really any doubt in your mind?"

"Not really," he admitted. "We're meant for each other."

"We are," agreed Sophie.

"Alana and Mutt will have to argue over who gets to be ring bearer," Samson pointed out.

"Alana does have experience . . ." Sophie pointed out.

"Fair enough," Samson said. "Sorry, Mutt."

Mutt wagged his tail, happy just to be included in the conversation.

"Come on," said Sophie. "Let's finish preparing for the party of the century. It's not every day your daughter turns one. Or every day you ask someone to be your wife."

"And she accepts." Samson grinned and pulled her in for another kiss before he put his arm around Sophie and the family headed home together.

THE END

THE JOFFE BOOKS STORY

We began in 2014 when Jasper agreed to publish his mum's much-rejected romance novel and it became a bestseller.

Since then we've grown into the largest independent publisher in the UK. We're extremely proud to publish some of the very best writers in the world, including Joy Ellis, Faith Martin, Caro Ramsay, Helen Forrester, Simon Brett and Robert Goddard. Everyone at Joffe Books loves reading and we never forget that it all begins with the magic of an author telling a story.

We are proud to publish talented first-time authors, as well as established writers whose books we love introducing to a new generation of readers.

We won Trade Publisher of the Year at the Independent Publishing Awards in 2023. We have been shortlisted for Independent Publisher of the Year at the British Book Awards for the last four years, and were shortlisted for the Diversity and Inclusivity Award at the 2022 Independent Publishing Awards. In 2023 we were shortlisted for Publisher of the Year at the RNA Industry Awards.

We built this company with your help, and we love to hear from you, so please email us about absolutely anything bookish at feedback@joffebooks.com

If you want to receive free books every Friday and hear about all our new releases, join our mailing list: www.joffebooks.com/contact

And when you tell your friends about us, just remember: it's pronounced Joffe as in coffee or toffee!

ALSO BY EMMA BENNET

HER PERFECT HERO
THE GREEN HILLS OF HOME
THE ONE THAT GOT AWAY?
STARSTRUCK
FALLING IN LOVE AT NIGHTINGALE FARM
A CHRISTMAS TRUCE
THE BABY PLAN